THE NEW FOREST.

A NOVEL.

BY THE

AUTHOR OF "BRAMBLETYE HOUSE," &c.

————"This boy is forest-born,
And hath been tutored in the rudiments
Of desperate studies."

AS YOU LIKE IT.

IN THREE VOLUMES.

VOL. I.

LONDON:

HENRY COLBURN, NEW BURLINGTON STREE

1829.

THE NEW FOREST.

CHAPTER I.

―――――――― Are not these woods
More free from peril than the envious Court ?
And this our life, exempt from public haunt,
Finds tongues in trees, books in the running brooks,
Sermons in stones, and good in every thing.

SHAKSPEARE.

ON the southern verge of the New Forest in
Hampshire, and at no great distance from the sea,
stands a large and populous village, to which,
for special reasons of our own, we shall assign
the fictitious appellation of Thaxted. Its situation and appearance were much more picturesque than might have been expected from
its vicinity to the sea, an element which, in our

northern latitudes, generally imparts a sterile
and unlovely character to the contiguous shores,
either preventing altogether the growth of
trees, or giving such a stunted, warped, and
cankered appearance to those that struggle
against the chalky soil and the stormy winds,
as to make them rather disfiguring than ornamental to the scenery. Such was not the
case at Thaxted, which was sufficiently removed from the great landscape-spoiler to be
beyond the reach of its baneful influence, and
yet near enough to derive from it all those
scenic embellishments which so eminently en-
hance the beauty of a rich land view, by affording occasional glimpses of the gleaming sea, or
a white sail, caught beneath the boughs of
noble trees, athwart the undulating hollows of
the intervening downs, or over an enclosed and
cultivated level. The village stood upon the
extreme edge of a heath, not of such extent
as some of those which, forming spacious openings in the interior of the New Forest, are
extensive enough to deserve the name of—

> "Vast savannas, where the wand'ring eye,
> Unfixed, is in a verdant ocean lost;"

and yet sufficiently large to give breadth, distance, and picturesqueness, to the surrounding
scenery. Its opposite extremity was bounded by
the Forest, forming woody bays and promon-
tories, alternately receding from, and advancing
into, the heath; now opening upon some deep
dark vista, athwart whose distant gloom the
deer were occasionally seen to bound, or from
which a timber-wain, in Hampshire called a
tug, was slowly emerging, under the efforts of
a numerous team of oxen;—now throwing forward some prominent grove so far upon the
open land, that the tuftings of its noble trees
fell into rich masses of light and shade, relieved
by the umbrageous back-ground of the Forest.
Nor was the heath itself by any means so forlorn or dreary an object as might be supposed.
Its broken surface, tufted with every variety of
furze, fern, and other wild plants, and presenting here and there the red ochreous banks of a
road that wound through it, was tinted with the
rich harmonious hues that a painter loves: detached clumps of trees, breaking its monotony,
served to unite its woody boundaries with its
area; while a large sheet of water that occu-

pied its centre, was nearly bisected by a long
projecting tongue of land, upon which, especially in the sunny evenings of summer, might
be seen groups of cattle, or forest mares with
their foals, sending their long shadows athwart
the golden bloom of the little lake. The view
from the opposite side of the gentle eminence
on which the village stood, though totally dissimilar, was scarcely less attractive—the eye
passing over enclosed corn-fields, pastures, and
meadows, till it reached the Isle of Wight, the
insularity of which not being perceptible to the
eye, gave to the intervening Channel the appearance of an extensive lake bounded by rug-
ged cliffs and distant mountains.

A clump of lofty elms and lime-trees, branch-
less for some distance from the ground, but
tufting over luxuriously at top, formed an
arch across the road leading to the village,
around which numerous flights of pigeons were
generally to be seen wheeling and careering;
while beneath its aperture might be discerned
the low spire of the church embosomed in foliage.
Athwart the straggling irregular central road
of Thaxted, dignified by the name of the High-

street, hung the sign of the chief inn, exhibiting a most bellipotent Saint George on a fiery
white horse, having obviously the best of it in
a conflict with a portentous green dragon, who
seemed to be complaisantly opening his mouth
for the express purpose of swallowing his ad-
versary's javelin. The building to which this
flaring daub was prefixed, was an ancient low
edifice, constructed with solid timbers blacken-
ed on the outside, the interstices being plaster-
ed and white-washed. A sharp-pointed gable,
fretted with half-decayed oak wood, crowned
the front; and the roof was of large sand-stones,
covered with moss and house-leek, from the
midst of which issued a ponderous red brick
chimney, placed edgeways, and surmounted
with numerous ragged mouldings. The upper
story projected over the lower, and the cornice
that divided them had sunk considerably on
one side, without, however, appearing to have
injured the general solidity of the building,
which, humble as it was, constituted the most
important structure in the High-street.

In passing the irregular assortment of barns,
sheds, shops, and houses, thatched, tiled, and

slated, that made up the straggling village, the
attentive traveller might observe, from the various inscriptions, that there seemed to be but
four names in the whole place, the two first exhibiting the unmeaning monosyllables of Wicks
and Stubbs, and the remaining two the more
rural compounds of Penfold and Haslegrove,
which, with various baptismal distinctions, were
perpetually alternated and interchanged; while
a physiognomist would have been tempted to
imagine, from the similarity of the faces surrounding him, that the owners of these four
appellations had successively intermarried until
the whole village had become, as it were, one
numerous family.   They who have derived their
notions from the golden age or the patriarchal
times, might dream that such a mutually connected society, inhabiting so beautiful and sequestered a retreat, would form an united
brotherhood of peace and love; while they who
contemplate our peasantry, " as truth will paint
them, and as bards will not," will not widely
err in forming a very different conclusion.   In
most large families, indeed, the claims of con-
sanguinity are too apt to be forgotten in op-

posing interests, and the consequent feelings of
jealous rivalry; in which respect, the greater
part of the inhabitants of Thaxted, " a little
more than kin and less than kind," offered no
exception to the general rule. Towards the
end of the village the road branched off in two
directions round a little green, furnished with a
finger-post, of which, according to the laudable
practice of semi-barbarous England, one of the
boards was broken off, and the other rendered
totally illegible; while a milestone on the opposite side of the road was equally unservice-
'able, from its figures having been carefully
punched out and obliterated. In front of the
green stood the stocks, the neglected state of
which attested either the orderly habits of the
villagers, or the remissness of the constable;
and behind this crumbling machine was a pool
of muddy water, termed the horse-pond, on the
poached margin of which might usually be seen
six or eight ducks, performing their toilet with
busy beak, and now and then detaching a
feather from their plumage, which was lazily
wafted by the wind to join those that fringed
the opposite bank.

Our history commences on a Sunday, on the afternoon of which the villagers of Thaxted, who, like most other Sabbath idlers of humble life, often found the unemployed hours hang rather heavy upon their hands, were divided into two knots, one of which, including most of the women and old men, went. to attend the funeral of old Isaac, one of their own body, canvassing his age, which was a matter of some doubt, and the little property he had left behind him, which seemed to be involved in equal uncertainty; while the other party, embracing the younger portion of the rustic community, betook themselves to the George Inn, to await the arrival of the London coach, which generally passed through about this hour. Nothing could more strongly mark the vacuity of the day, and the listlessness of the assemblage, than the lounging, lazy interest with which they awaited the appearance of the well-known vehicle, though they expected not that it should bring them any thing new, and they had repeatedly collected upon previous Sundays, at the same spot, at the same hour, to witness the driving up of the same coach, which, as

it did not change horses at Thaxted, seldom
stopped more than three or four minutes at
the George. At length it came in sight, passed
under the arch of trees to which we have already alluded, blessed the eyes of such dwellers
in the High-street as were drawn to the windows by the sound of the horn, and finally drew
up at the George, when the spectators, who had
been waiting so long for the information, were
enabled to ascertain once more, that it was driven
by Ned Davis as usual, was drawn by the four
customary horses, and conveyed no passenger,
either inside or out, whose appearance was calculated to excite the least attention. Fortunately, however, for the gazers, something new
was at last discovered, which effectually prevented their dispersion. A portion of the iron
binding, or tyre, had been detached from one of
the wheels, and the coach could not safely proceed until it had been replaced. A board upon
the very next house but one announced that its
occupant was—" John Stubbs, Horse-farrier,
Bullock-leech, and Blacksmith;" but it was
Sunday, the shop was shut up, and the rustic
Vulcan was not at home; though several voices

simultaneously declared that he would be sure
to be found down at the Cricketers.

The driver, as is usual with English coach-
men upon every emergency, cursed and swore
very heartily at the coach-cleaner, whose business it was to have examined the wheels; the
wielder of the whip being now-a-days much too
important a personage to attend to any depart-
ment of his own vehicle, beyond the driving it.
The gaping rustics busied themselves in conjectures as to where, when, and how the accident
had happened; until one of their body, a little
shrewder than his companions, suggested that
the truant iron must be somewhere; (a proposition which met with a ready assent and repetition
from the others,) and that it might be advisable
to dispatch a boy in search of it. This advice
was taken by the coachman, though not until he
had declared that any fool could have thought
of that expedient; and lest he should be anticipated in his farther measures by some other of
the bystanders, he immediately sent a second
lad in quest of Stubbs the blacksmith, and himself called lustily for Sam, the ostler of the
George; asking his opinion, when he appeared,

whether the wheel would go safely as far as the Mermaid, in case they could not find the missing iron.

" Ah, Master Davis," said Sam, patting and examining one of the horses, without even casting a glance upon the wheel; " so you 've put old Greyhound on the off-side, have you? He 'll go anywhere now; but I remember when nobody couldn't drive he nohow, without it was strait-haired Jack. Out-and-out, he was the most unrestless beast as ever I came nigh, all to nothing."

" D——n your chuckle-head !" cried the irritated coachman; "never mind old Greyhound, but look at the wheel. What d 'ye think of her ? Will she run on as far as the Mermaid ?"

" What, black Bess! are you there ?" continued Sam, tickling one of the leaders in the flank: " Ay, I 've rode she many a hundred mile when she were a poster; and I thought I had pretty well seen the end of her; but a horse with good bottom will do ye a deal of coach-work still, when the boy is taken off her shoulders."

A fresh volley of oaths from the coachman

testified how much his self-importance was
wounded by this dilatory and disrespectful pro-
ceeding of the ostler, and some of the passengers began to manifest strong symptoms of impatience; when, to the satisfaction of all parties,
the lad who had been sent in search of the
blacksmith, was seen approaching with John
Stubbs by his side; who, however, to judge by
his leisurely pace, was no great friend to expeditious proceedings.   When he at length reached the scene of inaction, and understood the nature of the accident, he very deliberately took
off his Sunday-coat, put on his spectacles, and
having minutely examined the wheel, and repeatedly shaken his head, he at length drawled
out—" Why, Master Davis, this be a pretty
baddish bit of a job, baint it ?"

" Will she go on as far as the Mermaid ?"
cried the coachman, pettishly.

" Na, that she won't, without I gi' her three
or four long screws."

" Well, then, set to work, man; and don't
stand there staring and jawing."

" Ay, ay, Master Davis, I always makes
quick work of it when once I begins;" and so

saying, he began slowly to put on his coat again.

"What the devil are ye up to!" bawled the coachman; "isn't this your shop?"

"Ay, but I left the key on't down at the Cricketers, when Bill called me away in such a hurry. Howsomever, I shall be back in ten minutes."

At this certainty of a fresh delay, one of the outside passengers exclaimed in a calm voice, and with a somewhat precise and formal manner, —"Coachman, this will be a tedious affair; by sitting here I shall certainly lose my time, and I may possibly lose my temper; there is no reason why I should do either: I will therefore get down, and remain at Thaxted. Please to give me my luggage."

As the coachman opened the boot, and drew out the traveller's small portmanteau, he endeavoured to propitiate him with that mollifying language, which is usually prompted by the anticipation of the valedictory fee. "No wonder gemmen should be vexed, 'twas enough to provoke the Devil himself; but 'twasn't no fault of his 'n, and might have happened to e'er a

coach in all England. He was unkimmon
sorry, and would take good care that Bill, the
coach-cleaner, should be properly mulked for it.
He had never been ten minutes behind time
afore since he druv the Nelson." With these
excuses the traveller seemed to be quite satisfied, for he paid him so handsomely as to be
rewarded with thanks and a rapid touch of the
hat; but he had no sooner entered the George,
than the driver, dropping the shillings into his
jingling pocket, observed aloud, as a hint perhaps to his remaining passengers—" What
cursed nonsense it is for gemmen to go and put
theirselves in a passion about what nobody in
the world couldn't help!" However absurd
might be such conduct in a gentleman, it did
not by any means apply to his passenger, who
had not evinced an atom of ill-humour, nor did
it put any restraints upon his own temper, for
the long absence of the blacksmith occasioned
another return of his impatience, which as usual
found vent in a fresh explosion of oaths, mut-
tered, however, in a low voice, rather out of
respect towards his remaining passengers, one

of whom was a Quaker, than from any particular reverence for the Sabbath-day.

Leaving him thus to solace himself until the arrival of John Stubbs should put his vehicle in a condition to pursue its route, we will follow the passenger, who had carried his own portmanteau into the George, the inmates of which neither presented themselves to welcome him to their caravansary, nor to relieve him of his burthen. The traveller was a tall, handsome young man, whose open countenance, strong hazel eyes, and singularly fine features, wore an expression of remarkable, though a somewhat sedate, not to say grave benignity, mingled with a certain character of decision that indicated a self-thinking and independent mind. Neat as it was, almost to formality, his dress was not in accordance with any of the prevailing modes of the day; a circumstance which might be attributed either to his recent return from a foreign country, or to his contempt for the frivolities of fashion. He had been too much accustomed to wait upon himself to heed those little marks of inattention that signalized

his entrance into the George Inn, especially as
the sordid, cringing servility of the lower orders
in England presented itself to his eyes as a somewhat degrading characteristic of the country.
But when he had thrice rung the bell of the little
parlour into which he had made his way, without
obtaining any other answer than that afforded
by the echo of his own alarum, he was induced
to sound a peal which might be fairly construed
into an expression of some impatience. Tony,
to whom, in the absence of the family, the office
of waiter had been temporarily deputed, was
summoned from the coach-wheel by the din, and
the traveller beheld stalking into the parlour, a
gaunt, meagre clown, with cold-looking, lank
jaws, a long red nose, swinish eyes, and pig-
coloured hair, while his scanty Sunday jacket,
not reaching to his wrists, exhibited to advantage two raw hands, which he held dangling
before him, as if at a loss how to dispose of
them. In answer to the inquiries of the unexpected guest, Tony stated that his master,
together with his daughter Sally, who usually
officiated as waiter, were gone to attend old
Isaac's funeral; that he himself was their sole

representative for the time being; and that a
good dinner, a good bed, and every suitable
accommodation might be had at the George, so
long as the stranger should be pleased to remain.

"How far is it from Thaxted to Mr. Gideon
Welbeck's?" inquired the stranger.

"What! Master Welbeck of the Manor-
house, justice of the peace and quorum? Why,
by the road, us charges six mile, and it 's that
good ; but across the fields it baint barely five.
Phil Haselgrove, the postman, has walked it in
an hour and ten minutes afore now, but then
he be a mortal long legged 'un. 'Taint more
nor a mile from where the coach stops."

"I know it, and it was my intention to have
gone on thither, but Thaxted will suit me as
well; and at Thaxted, therefore, I-shall probably remain for some days."

"What! at the George, along with we?
Well, that 's kind o' ye; and hang me if I baint
glad on it, for our business has run cruel slack
o' late. You baint going to stay at his worship's then, at the Manor-house?"

"I know him not; I never saw him; how,
then, should I be going to stay at his house?"

" You 've got an affidavy, then, to make, or
to lodge an information, or to ax for a summons, or summat o' that sort.   It's no use to go
to he of a Sunday."

" I require nothing of the kind—nothing
whatever at his hands," said the stranger, in a
tone that seemed intended to discourage farther
interrogatories.

Tony, who although a perfect clown, and little
better than a simpleton, was neither deficient in
curiosity nor a certain degree of cunning, seeing
himself baffled in his direct attempts at pump-
ing out the motives of the guest's visit to Thaxted, endeavoured to effect his object by a confidential communication of his own opinions touching the aforesaid Mr. Gideon Welbeck, a process which he commenced after the following
fashion.   " Well, hang me! if I baint glad you
ha' nothing to do wi' he, for between ourselves,
Sir," and here he dropped his voice to a whisper, and looked as secret and important as his
vacant countenance would allow him,—" I say,
Sir, atwixt you and I, he 's a bigger negre
nor Squire Frampton's blackamoor, a grasping,
greedy, miserly old huncks !   Zooks ! I 've a

good mind to tell ye how I sarved he when they had me up afore un for poaching a hare."

" Which is the way to the Manor-house, across the fields ?" inquired the stranger, apparently not wishing to hear the story of the hare.

" Lord love ye ! ye would never find the way ; but old Ball's in the stable, I'll just clap he into our taxed-cart, and bowl ye over there soon as ever Sam Ostler has started the Nelson."

" I never use the limbs of animals when my own will serve the purpose. I shall walk ; which is the way ?" A decision in the look, manner, and voice of the stranger, declared much more impressively than any words could have done, that his purpose was unalterable; so that Tony, having given him full directions how to find the path across the fields, quitted the room, muttering to himself, " A proper rum chap ! queer brutes these Lonnoners ! Danged if I wouldn't stand half a pint o' beer to know what he wants wi' the Manor-house, when he has got nothing to say to Old Skinflint. Drat me, if I believe it ! I'll try he again. I've caught more cunninger woodcocks nor he afore now." With a full determination to entrap the visitant, he hurried back into the room, exclaiming, " I say, Sir, if ye walk along at a good slapping pace, ye 'll catch his worship jist as he comes back from aternoon church."—Instead of noticing this intimation, the stranger, who had apparently been deep in a reverie, inquired, " Pray is Miss Welbeck staying at the Manor-house ? Has she returned from Southampton ?"

" Ay, that she is, and I warrant is at church wi' the justice this here very moment. Lord love ye ! there wouldn't be no bearing the old tyrant, if it wor 'n't for she : she 's no more like he, than Squire Frampton's racing filly 's like our raw-boned Ball in the stable. She do a mort o' good in these parts, and is almost as much loved as his worship is hated ; but, howsomdever, it don't become poor folks to speak ill of their betters, and he a justice o' the peace. Many people say she be as handsome as she be koind and generous-like ; but, Lord ! you 'd say she was but a poor spindle-shanked kind of body, if ye saw her by the side o' Molly Stubbs !"

The stranger took up his hat and quitted the apartment, without waiting to hear any farther illustrations of Miss Welbeck's style of beauty ;

when Tony, putting his forefinger to his nose, winking one eye, and doing his best to twist his sheepish features into a knowing look, whispered to himself, " Wheugh ! master ! I 've found you out, have I, for all so cunning as ye thought yourself ?   Ecod ! ye can't cheat Tony so easily.   I smelled a rat all the time, danged if I didn't ! but the old fox won't gi' his daughter and his fortin to none less than a lord or a baronite, I can tell ye.   Hang'd if I wouldn't stand a quart any day towards cheating him, and getting Miss Emily fairly out o' his clutches.   I would, danged if I wouldn't !"   Chuckling to himself at the thought of thus wreaking his revenge upon the obnoxious justice, who had called him to account for poaching a hare, Tony hastened back to the disabled wheel of the coach, which had almost excited as much interest in his vacant mind, as the unexpected visit of the stranger.

The latter, meanwhile, following the instructions he had received, discovered the path across the fields, and pursuing his route with a youthful vigour which might have done credit to Phil Haselgrove himself, emerged in little more

than an hour into the high road, along which
he had scarcely proceeded three or four hundred yards, when he beheld the entrance to the
Manor-house.   To spare the expense of a gate-
keeper, the lodge, no longer tenanted, had been
suffered to fall into decay, though the gate
itself was kept in repair for the purpose of
excluding cattle.   Pushing it open, the stranger
entered what had once been a spacious and
stately park, but which now wore a forlorn appearance of neglect and abandonment, where it
had not been intentionally disfigured to answer
the sordid purposes of its present proprietor.
Some of the recently-felled ornamental timber
was still lying upon the ground in melancholy
and unsightly confusion, and the sheet of water
in which they had once been proudly reflected,
was now become a wilderness of reeds and
rushes.   A large gravel-pit had been opened to
supply materials for a new road, for which the
interest of the justice had recently obtained an
Act of Parliament, partly with the view of thus
deriving an immediate profit from its formation,
and partly in the belief that it would ultimately
increase the value of his estate.   Slopes and

pastures, over which deer had once bounded, were now ploughed up and planted with potatoes; other portions were enclosed with hurdles, and let out to the neighbouring farmers for sheep or cattle feeding; every thing attested that this once fair and goodly domain had fallen into the possession of a man to whom it was not endeared by any hereditary associations, and who had a much keener eye to his own interest, than to the preservation of those picturesque, but unproductive beauties, which had once conferred celebrity upon the park of the Manor-house.

While the stranger stood gazing upon this scene, rendered perhaps more desolate, or, at least, more sordid, in its appearance from occasional marks of occupancy, than if it had exhibited signs of a total dereliction; an old peasant, seated on a shady bank beside him, exclaimed, as he respectfully touched his hat, " Ah, Sir, this be another guess sort of a place now from what I recollect it when the old Squire lived at the Manor-house. 'Twas a sad loss to the neighbourhood when he died off, and the estate came to Justice Welbeck, who was but a distant relation. It's a sad pity, baint it, Sir, to see such a fine place all cut to pieces and transmogrified, as a body may say, till it looks more like Boldre-Heath or No-man's-walk, than the manor-house park?"

"Why, my good friend," replied the stranger, with a benevolent smile, "surely it is more useful now than it was before. All land that will repay the expense ought to be cultivated—this seems to be a good soil, therefore it is right to cultivate it. Is it not better that so large a piece of ground, instead of being withdrawn from the community to pamper the pride of an individual, or furnish an occasional haunch of venison for the riot of his friends, should thus be made to contribute towards the formation of public roads, and supply sustenance for the poor?"

"Anan, Sir! I don't see how that argufies. Thirty years ago, I were gamekeeper to the old Squire; and I wouldn't gi' a quid of tobacco to see a park that hasn't plenty of preserves in it for game, and a good herd o' deer."

"And I, my friend, should be glad to see every park in the kingdom enclosed and planted, that it might support human beings, rather than beasts and birds, and become a scene of peace, industry, and plenty, instead of an arena for the warfare of keepers and poachers."

" Very like, Sir, very like: but these be new-fangled notions, such as I never heard of afore in all my born days, and I ha' lived a goodish bit, too! Cut down the covers, and plough up the preserves, quotha! what would come o' all the game, I should like to larn? A pretty rig, truly!" So saying, he passed through the gate into the high road, without touching his hat on parting from such a suspicious personage as an avowed enemy to pheasants and partridges, and the stranger pursued his way along the drive that led up to the mansion. It was level and in good order, for in a neighbourhood infested with smugglers and poachers, the road to the residence of the principal magistrate was sure to be in pretty constant use; but the untrimmed borders were rank with weeds and nettles, while the shrubberies and the plantations around the mansion had been suffered to shoot up into a wild overgrowth, which had obliterated the walks that once serpentined among them. The house itself, an extensive and venerable brick pile, seemed to have been built at different times, and in various tastes: high crocketed gables, surmounted with carved tabernacles, being intermingled with round and square castellated towers, while the pointed gothic windows alternated with projecting casements, overhung by fretted architraves. The whole building was in good repair, though the greater part of it was shut up, only that portion which looked out upon the garden appearing to be inhabited. In vain, however, did the stranger peer up at the windows to catch a glimpse of any of the inmates; nothing seemed to be moving within the dwelling, and the only signs of occupancy which presented themselves on the outside, were three cows standing in the shade, close under the walls of the building, and two sorry, lean coach-horses, haltered to the paling in the stable-yard. From the latter circumstance, the observer concluded that the family had returned from afternoon church, but he could perceive no servants moving about, not a single face at any of the windows; all was still, silent, and motionless, a circumstance which, in combination with the deserted state of the greater part of the building, imparted to the whole scene a singularly forlorn appearance.

" And this is the residence of Emily Wel-beck," said the stranger to himself; " she did not exaggerate when she described to me its melancholy character. There are some who cannot gaze upon a ruined castle without feel-ings of sadness; to me, it is the most cheer-ing spectacle in the world, as an evidence that peace and liberty have triumphed over the strong holds of the feudal system; nor am I less pleased to witness the decay of these stately man-sions, erected by the feudality of wealth ; for the downfall of one overgrown family, cannot but assist the advancement of many; and the bloat-ed possessions, or inordinate power of indivi-duals, only tend to impoverish the community, at the same time that they generally entail misery upon their possessors. It is of more con-sequence to extend human happiness, than to preserve these cumbrous piles, not seldom built up by the spoiler and the oppressor; and their dilapidation, therefore, is to me, a pleasing

proof, that the structure of our civil society
is daily receiving an accession of strength
and improvement. If people would contemplate moral, instead of physical beauty, they
would find no sight so pleasing as the pros-
tration of ancient castles, the destruction of
wealth's useless palaces, and the breaking up
and division of inordinate domains.—Poor
Emily! this must be an uncongenial dwelling-
place for thee."

So saying, the soliloquiser walked two or
three times round the lonely building, though
at some distance from it, occasionally venting
observations of the same tendency with those
which we have recorded; but as he could not
obtain a glimpse of a single inmate, though
he failed not to examine every window that
remained unbarricadoed, he at length quitted
the spot, again traversed the park, which, but
for the remaining clumps of noble trees, would
have rather resembled the purlieus of an extensive farm, and regaining the path across
the fields, returned to Thaxted at a much
more leisurely pace than when he had been
winning his way to the Manor-House.

CHAPTER II.

He who with pocket-hammer smites the edge
Of luckless rock or prominent stone, disguised
In weather-stains, and crusted o'er by Nature
With her first growths—detaching by the stroke
A chip or splinter—to resolve his doubts;
And with that ready answer satisfied,
The substance classes by some barb'rous name,
And hurries on; or from the fragments picks
His specimen, if haply intervein'd
With sparkling min'ral, or should crystal cube
Lurk in its cells—and thinks himself enrich'd,
Wealthier, and doubtless wiser than before!

WORDSWORTH.

HENRY MELCOMB, the stranger whom we
have thus conducted back to the George Inn,
was the adopted son of Captain Tenby of the
Royal Navy, who, when his young charge was
only two or three years old, had carried him
out to Canada, the frigate he commanded being

appointed to that station, and had placed him
under the guardianship of his wife, then residing at Montreal. This lady, having no children
of her own, cheerfully performed for her young
charge all the duties of a mother; and her benevolence, as is usual in most cases where that
virtue is called into exercise, found its own
reward; for the benefits she conferred, while
they kindled gratitude in their object, awakened
such a warm affection in herself, that she soon
loved the child as much as if it had been her
proper offspring, and blessed the chance that had
thus removed the principal source of their unhappiness, by providing them with a recipient for
their mutual affections, when they had abandoned all hope of possessing any direct issue.

As the faculties of the boy expanded, he became more especially endeared to his protectors,
by the innate generosity of his disposition, the
fervency of his gratitude to themselves, and
the unbounded affectionateness of his noble
heart; which, even at that early age, seemed to
overflow with love and kindness towards all
those that came within the sphere of its influence.
Most unfortunately for Henry, at the very

moment when his ductile mind was ready to
receive that durable impress which stamps the
future character, death deprived him of the invaluable friend who, without any of the mater-
nal ties, had so well discharged the duties of a
mother. Shortly after this privation he was sent
to school, where he had remained about a year
and a half, when, in an evil hour, the Captain
became smitten with the charms of a handsome
though vulgar and illiterate American widow
settled at Montreal, and married her. With
the exception of her beauty, which was her only
recommendation, she was in every respect
totally dissimilar from his first wife, and
Henry soon found a painful difference in the
treatment he experienced. Cold, sordid, and
selfish, the second Mrs. Tenby only beheld
in him a rival claimant for that fortune which
had been her sole inducement to marry, and
of which the ill-health of her husband seemed to promise her no very distant acquisition; under which impression it soon became
her object to deprive the child, if possible, of
the Captain's affections, by representing him
as totally unworthy of his favour, and every

way disqualified from becoming his heir.   During her husband's frequent and long absences
in the performance of his professional duty, she
endeavoured, by every species of neglect, and
even cruelty and oppression, to provoke Henry
into some such betrayal of passion or disobe-
dience, as might justify her complaints, and
promote her secret views.   But although, as
was very natural, he showed little or no regard
for his new mother, and evinced an occasional
sense of this tyranny and injustice, so far as
she herself was concerned; nothing could ever
shake his unbounded gratitude and loving duty
towards his father, for such he always termed
the Captain.   Disappointed in obtaining any
real ground of accusation against the boy, she
was so far overcome by her sordid disposition—
for she had not been originally unprincipled,
as to trump up fictitious charges, supporting
them by asseverations not less circumstantial
than unfounded.   The Captain, who was a clear-
sighted man, and soon discovered that he had
made a sad mistake in the choice of his second
wife, detected at once the falsehood of her cri-
minations, and the motives that had prompt-

ed them; and being not less decisive than penetrating, he compelled her, though not without considerable domestic discomfort to himself, to abandon this ungenerous line of conduct, whenever his public duty allowed him to reside on shore. This, however, was only occasionally; and after a few intervals of this nature, his frigate was so suddenly ordered to India, that he had no time to settle any new arrangements for the protection of his adopted son, though he took care to make his will, and deposit it with a friend before he left Montreal.

Shattered and weakened by previous ill-health, Captain Tenby soon fell a victim to the enervating effects of an eastern climate, and his widow had no sooner learned his death, than she hastened, with more anxiety about her anticipated gains, than regret for her recent loss, to examine the will. It disappointed her much as to the amount of the property left behind him, but infinitely more so in the appropriation of it; for her own share was restricted to a hundred pounds a-year, while the remainder, which, however, did not exceed three or four hundred a-year more, was bequeathed to his adopted son, Henry Melcomb. By this unequal division, her previous animosity against the youth was so aggravated, that she determined to lose no opportunity of wreaking her revenge, until the expiration of his minority should legally withdraw him from her clutches; a resolution which her authority as sole executrix, for such she had been inadvertently appointed, empowered her in many instances to perform. Under the pretext that their narrow income would not afford a school education, she withdrew him from the seminary at which he had been placed, and leaving him to prosecute his studies in whatever way he chose, or to neglect them altogether, she consoled herself for the testamentary mal-treatment she had experienced from her husband, by directing a constant though petty system of persecution and annoyance against his adopted son.

This was a situation which must inevitably have ruined both the head and heart of Henry, had he not been gifted with a patient, virtuous, and amiable temperament, proof against the seductions of pleasure or vice, and utterly un-

susceptible of any rancorous or revengeful feeling; at the same time that his fine intellect,
hungry for the acquisition of knowledge, found
in the spontaneous completion of his own education a resource and a delight which almost
atoned for the hardship of his forlorn and solitary lot.—A self-educated man, if he be at the
same time acute and reflective, possesses many
advantages over the regularly-drilled pupil of
the schools. In seminaries and colleges, where
it is the system to cultivate the head and neglect
the heart, the minds of our youth, without the
smallest regard to their respective tendencies,
are all thrown together into the same classical
mould; years are devoted to the drudgery of
the dead languages, that is to say, to the acquisition of sounds instead of the expansion of
ideas—to the making of linguists instead of
thinkers; the leaves of the tree of knowledge
are more considered than its fruit; models are
set before the students, that they may be ser-
vilely and uninquiringly copied;—to resemble
their predecessors, and thus render the general
literature of the country stationary, is the great
object of their ambition; and the result of all

this elaborate fettering of the free intellect is
the diffusion of an uniform, perhaps a graceful
learning, of which, however, the invariable characteristics are monotony, tameness, imitation.
Were our minds allowed to shoot out according
to their natural propensities; were we encou-
raged to think more for ourselves, and trust less
to the thoughts of others; to prefer sense to
sound; to learn our lessons by head rather
than by rote; we should doubtless witness much
extravagance and error; but there would be
infinitely more of character, of originality, of
genius. We should have a natural landscape,
in short, the more beautiful because wild and
unpruned, instead of clipped hedges, uniform
parterres, correspondent alleys, and trim gar-
dens, where " half the platform just reflects the
other."

Of the benefits to be derived from self-in-
struction, conducted by a powerful and inquiring mind, Henry, as he grew up, imbibed his
full portion, while he did not by any means
escape the disadvantages consequent upon a
want of comparison and collision with other and
more experienced intellects. Weeds had sprung

up with the flowers in the progress of his isola-
ted education. An innate impulse directed him
more earnestly towards the useful branches of
knowledge, especially where they could be rendered conducive to the melioration of his fellow-
creatures. He might be termed a natural
utilitarian, whose laudable aspirations for human improvement led him to undervalue such
literature as was merely ornamental, and to
think meanly of all pursuits that were not con-
tributary to his own philanthropic views, although these were frequently superficial or mistaken, and sometimes incapable of execution.
Owing to his utter exclusion from society, he
was totally deficient in tact. Such, indeed, was
his reverence for the majesty of truth, that no
earthly consideration would prompt him to compromise it; even its suppression seemed to him
to make so near an approach to its violation,
that he rarely concealed his thoughts; but, in
the sincerity of his honest heart, gave vent at
times to the most startling and heterodox pro-
positions, totally regardless what prejudices or
feelings he might wound, what hearers he
might astound and horrify. Of a naturally

sedate temperament, his own cheerless lot, his
sense of the miseries of his fellow-creatures, and
his intense conviction that by a little better
management among ourselves they might be
materially alleviated, had combined to invest
his character with a seriousness and a reflective
turn, seldom seen in youth. Hence he was
rather intolerant of bantering and levity—it
conduced to no useful purpose—it seemed out
of keeping with the real state of the world—
and an idle joke seldom failed to make him look
grave. He was a strict grammarian, because
he thought it of importance that men should be
accurate in the conveyance of their ideas; and
so acutely sensitive was he to errors, or even
vulgarisms of speech, that he scrupled not to
correct them upon the spot, whenever they
proceeded from individuals whose rank and
education ought to have secured them against
such lapses, although he passed them over in
the lower classes without notice, deeming their
ignorance a misfortune, not a fault. Conversant with books, rather than with men, and
accustomed to condense his thoughts into a
logical form, his own conversation was apt to

assume a syllogistic or laconic phraseology, which might well be mistaken for affectation, though it was quite unpremeditated, and he himself was utterly unconscious that his discourse was liable to any such imputation.

To confess the truth, we have a vehement suspicion, that as our history proceeds, the reader will be occasionally prone to apostrophize Henry Melcomb as a prig, a pedant, a pragmatical fellow, and perhaps to bestow upon him still more derogatory epithets, not duly considering how fairly his little oddities and peculiarities, or even his more startling and indefensible opinions, may be attributed to the circumstances of his birth and education. Should our young friend be visited with any such petulant rebukes, we must submit to the infliction, cheering ourselves with the reflection, that we never meant to delineate a faultless monster, but to adhere as scrupulously to the truth as Henry himself would have done, had he been called upon to pourtray his own character. Whatever intermediate judgment may be passed upon his little failings, we trust that we shall ultimately insinuate him into the good

graces of all parties. His cup of life, even in
his childhood, had been filled with moral bit-
ters, which in their tonic effect had surprisingly
fortified and corroborated his mind. Ignorant
who were his parents, he had of course no known
relations; his only friend was snatched from
him at an early age; he was of a temperament
unusually affectionate, and in the want of more
immediate objects for its reception, his love
might be said to overflow upon the community
at large, although directed in an especial manner towards the poor and the lower orders,
who seemed in more urgent need of his good
offices.   By substituting for the sordid and
grasping selfishness which is now so carefully
instilled into our minds, a more expansive system of benevolence and mutual assistance, he
believed that the state of human society might
be very materially improved, and if in develop-
ing his undigested notions, he sometimes indulged in visionary or dangerous reveries, he
never recommended to others what he would
not have cheerfully performed himself; and
none could refuse him the praise of being
a most amiable and disinterested enthusiast,

though it might sometimes be truly asserted
that he was a mistaken one.

Some years after the death of Captain Tenby,
his widow, in order to be near a relation, removed to an infant settlement in one of the
American States, accompanied by Henry. Here
a new, and, to his inquiring mind, a peculiarly
interesting scene was opened to his observation.
He attended the public-meetings for the regu-
lation of the colony, took minutes of the proceedings, and in process of time acquired sufficient confidence in his own observations and
reflections to suggest, both orally and in writ-
ing, several improvements, most of which were
adopted, and procured for him the reputation of
being a sound thinker, and a singularly promis-
ing young man. Although his advancement
towards maturity rendered him independent of
his mother, for such he respectfully termed her,
however little she deserved the name, he continued to reside with her, subject to all the in-
flictions of her unconcealed dislike, which time
seemed rather to aggravate than diminish. Frequently did he expostulate with her upon the
unreasonableness of her aversion, in the hope

that he might conquer it by argument, though
he had failed to conciliate her esteem by a long
course of truly filial deference and attentions.
From the expressions which escaped her upon
these occasions, he discovered that the secret and
insuperable cause of her animosity was the unequal distribution of her husband's property;
an act of indignity and injustice to herself which
ever since his death had been rankling in her
sordid mind. Beyond the bare means of sub-
sistence, money was to Henry an object of supreme indifference, if not of contempt; and he
therefore hesitated not to declare that the disposition of the will was an unfair one, since he
had no legal or natural claim whatever upon the
Captain's bounty; professing at the same time
his fixed determination, so soon as he became of
age, to take the widow's portion for his own
share, which would be quite sufficient for all his
wants, and to make over to her in perpetuity
the larger income bequeathed to himself.

"What!" exclaimed one of his American
acquaintance, when he stated this intention to
him, " impoverish yourself for *her*, for the un-
feeling, unnatural woman who has ever hated

you, ever maltreated you, ever been your per-
secutor and oppressor since the Captain's death,
and who would previously have alienated him
from you by her infamous aspersions!"

"In the measure I propose, and which I
shall certainly carry into effect," replied Henry
calmly, "I do not consider what is due to her,
but what is due to myself, and to the memory
of Captain Tenby. It is not right that his
adopted son should be richer than his widow;
nor am I the less grateful for his generous kindness when I refuse to avail myself of it. One
of the Roman emperors said he would destroy
all his enemies by making them his friends.
I will endeavour to imitate his example, and
with whom can I more properly or delightfully
begin than with Mrs. Tenby? Money is of no
use unless where it can confer happiness—but
it confers no happiness upon me, therefore I
am no loser in parting with it. Or let us place
the syllogism thus—Money *is* of use where it
confers happiness; it can produce this effect
upon my father's widow, therefore it is desirable that she should have it."

The American turned round and walked away with a look of ineffable contempt, muttering to himself; " The boy's a pedant, I guess ; a born fool, little better than a nait'ral!"

Mrs. Tenby's feelings had been irritated and perverted by avarice, which was the ruling passion of her mind, but she was a shrewd and acute, and not originally an unprincipled woman. She knew that Henry never made a promise which he did not if possible perform; she had seen enough of his honest, straightforward, generous character, to believe him capable of carrying the meditated exchange into effect, without even being conscious of the sacrifice he was volunteering ; and the prospect of gratifying her darling propensity worked a sudden marvellous change in her conduct. Determined not to afford him the slightest pretext for retracting his pledge, even had he been so disposed, her demeanour now became as smooth, amicable, and insinuating as it had previously been churlish and morose. Henry, gratified even by the appearance of an affection to which he had so long been a stranger, was delighted beyond measure at the alteration, and

thought it impossible that he could ever have
made a happier disposition of his little fortune,
than by thus employing it to convert an enemy
into a friend.

The property was in the British funds.
Henry, as he approached the expiration of his
minority, signified his intention of residing in
England, and Mrs. Tenby resolved to accompany
him, assigning as a reason, her anxiety to visit
a brother of her first husband, who was settled
at Southampton, although her real motive was
the fear of being separated from her nominal
son, until the contemplated pecuniary arrangement in her favour should be legally completed.
This had been effected some little time previously to the commencement of our history,
and it is gratifying to record that the mother's
mind, (for such we shall continue to call her,)
thus set at ease upon the great object which was
always nearest to her heart, was not again visited by any of those unamiable feelings which she
had previously cherished. Of Henry's understanding, indeed, she formed an immeasurably
lower estimate than before, for she had always
thought him an intelligent young man; but

such was now her opinion of the goodness and
generosity of his heart, that she became as
much attached to him as the coldness of her
own nature would allow. Perhaps it was rather compassion than regard that thus drew
her towards him, for believing that he must be
almost simplewitted and imbecile thus to bestow
the greater part of his fortune upon one who
had certainly not acquired any particular claim
to his liberality, she feared lest he should suffer
the remainder to be wheedled away from him,
and the very teeth to be drawn from his head,
by any artful or insinuating associate who should
once find the way to his heart. To guard him
against such dangers by the interposition of her
own superior sagacity, it was agreed that they
should continue to live together, and in a moment of solitary and unprecedented weakness,
she even consented to take such a trifling additional sum out of his scanty income for his
board and lodging, that, according to her own
subsequent declaration, she was sure to be a
loser by the arrangement at the year's end.

Early on the morning after Henry's arrival
at Thaxted, an ambiguous-looking personage

bustled into the yard of the George-inn, whistling as he entered, and then calling with a loud
and cheerful voice for the landlord, Sam Ostler,
Tony, and pretty Sally, apparently indifferent
whether he procured the attendance of one or
all, so that his summons were promptly answered. We have termed his appearance ambiguous on account of his dress, which consisted
of a fustian jacket and trowsers, and a seal-skin
cap, while he had a well-laden wallet slung
across his shoulders, and a stout crutch-headed
staff in his hand. He had neither dog nor gun
to justify the suspicion of his being a sportsman,
nor was it indeed the season for such recrea-
tions : he was past the meridian life, and though
his look and deportment did not indicate any
very polished degree of gentility, there was a
freedom and self-possession, not to say a slight
air of importance in his manner, which showed
him to be superior to his homely habiliments,
and might lead a keen observer to infer at the
first glance that he was in independent circumstances, and by no means unconscious of the
fact. The individual thus described, was Mr.
Mark Penguin, originally a tradesman, and

latterly a merchant at Southampton, who having made a fortune during the war by privateer-
ing, according to his own version of the matter,
but rather by his extensive smuggling transactions, according to the insinuations of the cen-
sorious world, had lately retired from business,
upon the conclusion of the peace, and had become a resident in the neighbourhood of Thaxted, where he had purchased a house and estate.
Like others who have suddenly exchanged a
life of business and excitement for one of inoccu-
pation and repose, he soon found the misery of
enjoying himself (as it is termed;) but being of an
active and intelligent mind, he was neither long
in discovering the cause of his discomfort and
ennui, nor in providing a remedy for it.   It was
indispensable, he maintained, to the happiness
of every unemployed man, that he should have a
hobby, and he determined that his own should
be the study and practical illustration of geology.
He had obtained some smattering of this science
when in business, and he possessed little more
now, though he had since been an extensive pur-
chaser, and a diligent, if not judicious, reader
of books upon this subject; but making up in

enthusiasm what he wanted in knowledge, he
devoted himself to the pursuit *con amore*, purchased minerals, fossils, specimens, knick-knacks,
and trumpery of all sorts for the formation of a
museum, to which purpose he had devoted the
largest room in his house; generally arrayed
himself every fine morning in his geological
dress, such as we have described it; and having
duly deposited a hammer in his wallet, together
with two or three books of geological engravings,
in order that he might sit down and look them
over when he was weary, or be instantly enabled
to classify and name whatever specimens he
might be so fortunate as to encounter, he sallied
forth towards the lime and marl-pits, or the
cliffs, knocking upon the head every suspicious
stone that he met with by the way, and stopping
to examine every bank or excavation, in order
that he might pronounce upon the strata of
which it was composed. In these excursions
he could hardly be a loser, for they kept both
his body and mind in good health; and if he
picked up nothing worth having, which was
almost invariably the case, he at least got rid of
the time, which to him was so much clear gain.

Early as it was on the morning when he entered
the George-inn, he had already walked several
miles, and his wallet being laden with flints of
sly aspect, and lime or other stones which looked very much as if they contained some hidden
treasures, he had made for the caravansary in
the hope of recreating himself with some syllabubs, for the nice manufacture of which,
pretty Sally, the innkeeper's daughter, had
obtained no inconsiderable portion of village
fame.

Tony, the first individual who answered his
general summons, knew the visitant, as well as
his habitual occupations, and having always a
shrewd suspicion in his mind, that a man who
could voluntarily pass the whole morning in
breaking stones, a drudgery to which the lowest
paupers are condemned, must be nearly as much
cracked as the flints that were subjected to his
hammer, he could not suppress a little jerk of
his shoulders, and a smothered chuckle, as he
approached.   To prove his respect, however, he
pulled down his head by a lock of his pig-co-
loured hair, and with a look and tone, neither
of which were entirely divested of a sneering

expression, though he endeavoured to be as grave as possible, he said, as he ushered him into the little parlour,

" You ha' been a breaking a mort o' stones, this morning, I reckon?"

" A good sportsman, Tony, knows where to find the game; and a clever geologist will seldom be at a loss for subjects for his hammer. My wallet, you see, is tolerably well filled, but my stomach is proportionably empty; wherefore, bring me quickly my morning's tiffin, some fresh syllabubs and a plate of biscuits." The foaming delicacies were speedily placed before him in long narrow glasses, when he commenced immediate operations upon his favourite refection, prefacing the process by his usual inquiry of—" Well, Tony, what news with you?"

" Why, thank ye kindly, Sir, no great matter o' news, except that us ha' got a strange gemman come to stay some time at the George."

" A strange gentleman!—some time—at the George, too! Do you call that no news?" exclaimed Penguin, who having no affairs of his own to look after, took a prodigious interest in those of others, and was, in fact, the busy-body

of the whole neighbourhood. "Who is he,
Tony? what's his name? do you know any
thing about him?" And the first syllabub
remained unfinished in eager expectation of the
reply.

"Know any thing about un? Doant I, Master Penguin?" answered the clown, putting his
long red finger to his nose, and winking one of
his pig's eyes. "Ecod! he thought to run his
rigs upon I, to come the old fox, but I pumped
'en finely; danged if I didn't!

"Did you so, Tony; and what might you
discover?"

"Why, sure as ever I stand here, him be
come a sweethearting a'ter Justice Welbeck's
daughter."

"What! a lover of my friend Emily! Impossible, Tony! She knows no stranger, poor
thing; and if she did, she would be too shy
and diffident to encourage him. Besides, if this
were his object, why should he stay here? He
would be nearer to the Manor-house at the
coast."

"Well, and him were a-going on to the coast,
warn't him, only Ned Davis rattled the tyer off

o' one o' the Nelson's wheels. *I* think it were
dine a-coming down Boldre Hill, and so he got
out here; ay, and do mean to stop here some
days."

" Some sick citizen, Tony, depend upon it,
who liked the appearance of our village, and
thought he might recover his health as well
here, as by inhaling the sea-breezes. Has he
the look of a valetudinarian ?"

" No! him don't look like a valet to ne'er-
a-one. Lord love ye! him be a gemman, I tell
ye."

" Perhaps he expects to live cheaper here
than if he went on to the coast; and sooth
to say, there is no small difference in the
charge for lodgings. Ay, ay, I dare say he
comes here from parsimony !"

" Not he; him do come here from Lunnun,
there baint a doubt o' that, for I axed Ned.
You may leave me alone, Master Penguin,
for finding out the right meaning o' things."

" Ay, Tony, and the wrong one too; and
therefore I should be glad to know why
you have formed the sapient conclusion, that
Miss Welbeck—but here comes talking Timo-

thy, from whom, I dare say, we shall get the long of the matter, though we cannot expect the short of it.—Good morning, landlord, good morning."

Tony retreated from the room with another pull of his lank hair, and a simultaneous scrape of his left foot upon the floor, leaving to his master, as in duty bound, the farther developement of the stranger's character and intentions; but that the reader may understand the singular jargon of the voluble Mr. Timothy Wicks, landlord of the George, it is necessary to premise that he was a bustling, loquacious, empty-headed, little man, who had originally been a waiter, and had succeeded to his present post of landlord, by marrying his predecessor's widow. His spouse had now for many years been dead, leaving him sole proprietor of the George; the accounts of which flourishing concern he would never have been able to keep, for he was totally uneducated, but for the assistance of his daughter Sally. Finding himself in tolerably easy circumstances, our *bourgeois* resolved at length to be *gentilhomme*, so far, at least, as education was concerned;

and, iu order that he might keep pace with
the march of intellect, he went over once a
week to attend the scientific lectures that
were given at a neighbouring town.—The Mechanics' Institutes, which, by inviting a large
class of the community to substitute intellec-
tual for sensual pursuits, must tend to raise
it in the scale of being, not less certainly than
to embalm the name of their founder as a
benefactor to the human race, had not, at
this period, been established. At the lectures
he attended, Tim Wicks, faithfully committing
to his memory all the hard words and technical
terms, which he considered to be the pith and
marrow of the whole matter, (although, in other
respects, he came away just as ignorant as he
went,) blurted them out upon all occasions
with a most ludicrous and acute misconcep-
tion of their meaning. This scientific mala-
prop sometimes changed his Babel dialect, according to the subject of the last lecture he
had heard; the only part of his discourse
that remained unvaried, being the fuss and
pucker with which he called about him, and
interlarded his disjointed gabble with orders

to Sally, cook, Sam ostler, and Tony, in the hope of persuading others, and perhaps himself, that the quiet, little-frequented inn of the George, was full of company, and involved in a consequent hubbub of business.

Amused by the absurdities of his character, attracted by Sally's syllabubs, and, perhaps, not altogether displeased to have a peep at her pretty face, Penguin seldom missed an opportunity in his rambles of turning into the parlour of the George-inn; and upon the present occasion, thus proceeded to commune with his host, who, having left the door of the room open, that he might both hear and observe what was passing within, bustled unceasingly about the chamber, now peeping out of the window into the road, now peering towards his own tap and stable-yard, and now busily whisking the dust from the furniture with a napkin which he held in his hand.

" Where's your pretty daughter, landlord? if I saw her, I should scold her for not having made her syllabubs so good as usual."

" Gone up to Doctor Dotterel's, Sir, to settle with the clerk. Pay as you go, that's my max-

imum; and I wish all my customers would act
upon the same square-root, and pay down, as I
do, down upon the fulcrum, Sir. It comes to
the same thing in the end, for the velocity's
always proportioned to the descent.—Syllabubs
not so good as usual? Like enough. Not made
by Sally to-day, but by crooked Martha, our
cook.—Sam ostler! gemman wants bay mare.—
You've seen crooked Martha, Sir—poor thing!—
good cook, but not quite a parallelobiped—sadly
out of the perpendicular—her momentum built
too much upon the diagonal. Why, Sir, a right
line, A. B. from her head to her foot, would
describe an angle of forty-five degrees;—no
beauty neither in the face: I call her my inclined plane. Hi! hi!—D'ye catch the focus?—
Tony! answer bell, back-parlour. Coming, Sir,
coming!—For my part, Sir, when I look at
Martha, standing as she does, and describing a
sort of spherical equilibrio, I often wonder how
she preserves her centre of gravity."

"I'm sure I find it difficult to preserve mine,"
said Penguin, smiling, "when I listen to your
learned discourse. You have been attending a
lecture upon mechanics, I presume?"

" Yes, Sir; monstrous clever man that Professor Pulley: told me many things I never heard afore; no inverse ratio about him, nothing of the sort; all rectilinear; quite a polygon of a man, and proves all his conundrums in the twinkling of a radii;—shows you the proper trigonometry of every thing at once, and that's what I like.—Sam ostler! gemman on the switch-tail horse.—Coming, Sir, coming!— Why, now, Sir, when you want to get up out of a chair, do you know why you draw your feet inwards, and rest upon their extreme axis? Why, to preserve the equilibrio, and have the centre of gravity right under you; and that's the reason why you do not fall slap backwards, as flat as a parallelogram. D'ye catch the focus? Ay, and the Professor proved to us— to be sure, he brings every thing point-blank to the fulcrum, that in walking you never take both legs off the ground at once, while you do so in running. Now that's a vertical truth,—a mathematical maximum, as I may say; and yet I never thought of it afore.—Tony! gemmen in the tap calling more beer.—Coming, Sir, coming!"

" Truly, landlord, you appear to have bene-
fited more than usual by your last lecture."

" Ah, Sir ! I am little better than a smatterer after all : haven't brought away half so much
as I ought. I wish you could have heard the
learned Professor describe a parabola, or show
us the trigonometry of the categorical curve,
and the Isausages wedge.—There's two bells
ringing at once ! Where can Sally be daudling?
I expected her back in the segment of a circle."

" I am disappointed myself at not seeing her,
no less than I am in the quality of the syllabubs. How comes on her love affair with the
young miller ?"

" Off and on, Sir, backwards and forwards;
always in a state of osculation, like the pendulum of our kitchen-jack : but I suppose the
problem will find its own lever some day or
other.—Coming, Sir, coming !"

" But, landlord, before you go, do tell me
what you know of the strange gentleman up-
stairs, and why he has taken up his abode at the
George ?"

" As to that, Sir, it's a vertical rule with
me never to pry into secrets, but to let every

axis revolve upon its proper impetus. No doubt he has his own momentum for coming here: for where there's a maximum there must be a minimum; but it wouldn't become me to be ferreting out his fulcrum just as he has come into the house. Little brass-plate under the handle of his portmanteau, with the name of Melcomb engraved upon it, but that may be all a sham segment, and turn upon a false pivot, after all. He seems a shy bird, and I doubt whether his object is altogether rectangular and horizontal right line — A B. — Coming, Sir, coming!—Always in a bustle at the George, early and late—for ever on the move—toilsome work—slaving, slaving, from morning till night!"

" Well, but landlord, have you not formed a notion as to the purport of this stranger's visit to Thaxted, for every one will be questioning me about it, and I should, at least, like to have a conjecture to offer ?"

" Why, Sir, mum's the word and no blabbing, that's my square-root: but, to say the truth, I have formed a little problem of my own. There has been a good deal of running lately

to the opposite coast among the free-trade gentlemen, and I have taken it into my head that
he has come down to do a little bit of business
upon the sly, and thinks, perhaps, he would be
less observed here than upon the coast. That's
my theorem of the matter, Sir; do ye catch the
focus?"

By this gentle periphrasis the landlord meant
to convey his impression that his inmate was
concerned in contraband trade; a business which,
during the war had been carried on to a considerable extent in that neighbourhood, though
he knew better than to apply harsh terms to
any species of smuggling in the presence of Mr.
Penguin. The latter was about to question
him farther as to the grounds of his opinion,
when he bolted out of the room, crying, " Coming, Sir, in the segment of a tangent! Sally!
where the dickens have you been ? I expected
you back in a momentum.—Glass brandy and
water in the Dolphin—cold, arout sugar.—Look
to the tap, Tony !—Sam, ostler ! saddle gemman's grey pony.—Coming, Sir, coming!"

CHAPTER III.

Mr. H. Your name is Pry, I think?

Pry. Yes, Sir; Jeremiah Pry, at your service.

Mr. H. An apt name: you have a prying temper.
I mean some little curiosity; a sort of inquisitiveness
about you.

Pry. A natural thirst after knowledge, you may call
it, Sir.   CHARLES LAMB.

PENGUIN, though not personally so loco-
motive as his bustling landlord, was of a disposition infinitely more prying and busy; his
mind was no more able to stand still than was
the body of Mr. Timothy Wicks; doing nothing was the hardest drudgery that could be
imposed upon him; it was the great object of
his present life to escape from it, and if he
could keep himself in a perpetual though vain
and useless pucker, like a squirrel in its rota-
tory cage, he was willing to compound with his

faculties, and sacrifice their progress to their
activity. No sooner did he find himself alone,
than he proceeded to decypher, for the fiftieth
time at least, the fulsome scrawlings upon the
parlour window, perfectly well disposed to
" accept a miracle instead of wit," could he
have made any such discovery; but as he observed nothing but the autographs and amatory
effusions with which he was already familiar,
he returned to his chair, and betook himself to
sundry conjectures touching the intelligence he
had received. Slight as was the foundation for
such a surmise, he felt convinced that the motive of the stranger's visit to Thaxted was some
important secret, and as his mind made as dead
and sure a point at any mystery, as does the
staunch spaniel at a concealed hare, he determined instantly to ferret it out if possible.
The notion of his being attached to Emily
Welbeck he treated as an idle emanation of the
brainless head of Tony, for he knew her to
be modest and reserved, almost to a morbid
bashfulness, while he believed her to have no
acquaintance beyond the immediate neighbourhood in which she lived. A remembrance, per-

haps, of his own former practices, induced him
to consider the landlord's suggestion as infinitely more plausible; but he felt, or at least
discovered, no sympathy whatever with his pre-
sumed brother contrabandist, since, in order
to avert the imputation which he knew to be
attached to his own character, he now affected
an ostentatious abhorrence of all similar mis-
demeanours, and talked loudly and angrily
against the smugglers with whom the neighbourhood was infested, though he never interfered
actively to prevent any of their proceedings.
While he was deliberating how he might best
pump the stranger, the individual in question
entered the parlour, when Penguin, who believed that the old adage of their being truth in
wine, extended to edibles and potables of every
description, saluted him with a cordial fami-
liarity, and pressed him so hospitably to assist in finishing the remaining syllabubs, that
Henry, who was of a singularly friendly and
accostible disposition, instantly acquiesced.—
" Mr. Melcomb, I believe," said Penguin, plying his spoon with renovated pleasure at the

thought that he had thus pinned down the subject of his experiment.

"That is my name," said Henry, somewhat surprised; "but I have not the honour of your acquaintance."

"Belong to the family of that name at Blackwater, in the north, of the county, I suppose?"

"I was not aware that any family of that name existed in Hampshire."

"Then you are doubtless one of the Melcombs, or Malcombs, of Cricklade, in Wiltshire?"

"They are equally unknown to me."

"There was an old Joel Melcomb,—warm Joe, we used to call him, for he was a rich old hunks—died at Southampton a few years ago."

"I never heard of him; and to save you farther trouble, I may as well inform you at once, as I used to declare to the good citizens of America, when they perpetually cross-questioned me, I neither know the birthplace nor the names of my parents."

"Humph!" said Penguin, concluding this was merely advanced to stop farther interrogatories, and feeling his curiosity rather stimu-

lated than repressed by such a suspicious declaration.   " You seemed to admit that your
name was Melcomb, talked of being in America ;
you are then an American, I suppose ?"

" I believe myself to have been born in England, though in what part I cannot tell you, for
I am myself ignorant of the fact ?"

" *Rather* a marvellous tale," said Penguin,
with an incredulous look, and an emphasis upon
the first word which seemed to betray a conviction that it was altogether a fabrication.
" Few people would like to make such a humiliating confession, especially to a stranger whom
they had never seen before."

" What other people may or may not like is
no rule to me.   *I* like truth, I hate unnecessary
mystery, and I see nothing humiliating in what
I have avowed.   In being the acknowledged son
of the highest nobleman, I should not feel myself
exalted ; nor should I hold myself degraded,
were it proved that I was the offspring of a
beggar."

" All right, all very right ; quite agree with
you, particularly in what you say about un-

necessary mystery; nothing like frankness and
candour among friends, we are all friends here,
under the rose." The last words being given
in a very significant tone, as if to inspire confidence in his auditor, and win him to a confession of his purpose in visiting Thaxted: Penguin, who now suspected him more than ever
of being engaged in some smuggling transaction, continued—" Beautiful nights, Sir, for
the trade, considering the season."

" On the contrary, the nights have been
remarkably dark and rather stormy ; no moon,
and not a single star to be seen."

" Well, those are beautiful nights, are they
not, for the *free-trade?* You understand me?
There has been a good deal of working lately.
Three crops of goods run ashore in the Miller's
Gap, not a hoop lost. Two poor smugglers
were shot, though, about a week ago, down by
the Rook Cliff."

" He who defrauds the Government, and
thereby the community at large, does a greater
wrong than the highwayman who stops and robs
an individual, in the exact proportion of one to

the whole nation. I am sorry for the smugglers you mention, as I am for all malefactors, but while laws exist they must be obeyed."

"True, true; all very right in a general way, but a little trifle of smuggling, you know, nobody objects to."

"I beg your pardon, Sir. I object to it, as I would to any other misdemeanour that combines certain fraud, falsehood, and duplicity, with contingent violence and bloodshed."

Finding that his companion did not by any means sympathize with the indulgent tone he had assumed towards the smugglers, in the hope of coaxing him into some sort of confession, Penguin quickly resumed his customary severity in speaking of such delinquents, acknowledged that there was good excuse for winking at their practices during the war, since they were very often highly beneficial to the nation; but added, that in a time of peace, they were not less unwarrantable than injurious, and ought unquestionably to be suppressed, as far as possible, by the strong and inexorable arm of law. In support of this singular distinction, suggested, probably, by his own mind, in vindication

of his own past conduct, he did not attempt to
advance any argument, for he found the flattering
unction too grateful to his soul, to run any risk
of having it rudely withdrawn. There are few
offenders who do not secretly attempt to vin-
dicate their own course of life by some such subtle casuistry; and if the individual in question
could persuade himself, that by smuggling during the war, and leaving it off at the peace,
(when he had made a handsome fortune,) he
had been all along acting patriotically, he was
surely quite right not to expose such a self-re-
conciling conviction to the hazard of a refutation. He would have taken it for granted, that
his companion's condemnation of the practice
had been merely assumed for the occasion as
well as his own; for he was by no means deficient in that shallow, worldly cunning, which
suspects the motives of others, and presumes
every man to be a rogue, till he has proved himself to be honest; but there was something so
frank, ingenuous, and unreserved in the look and
voice of Henry; truth was so visibly stamped
upon his fine open brow, that it was impossible,
even for the most mistrustful observer, to doubt

his sincerity. Still, however, he had not declared the purport of his visit to Thaxted, and
Penguin, deeming that the most likely method
to discover it, was to insinuate himself into his
good graces, stated himself to be a resident
in the neighbourhood, offered his services in
farthering the views of the stranger, whatever
might be their nature, and ended by inviting
him to become his companion in the remainder
of his morning's ramble, observing, that the weather was remarkably fine, and that he was well
acquainted with all the most picturesque scenery
in the vicinity.

Without entering into any detail of his motives for coming to the spot, Henry courteously
thanked him for his civility, and declaring that
he would gladly accompany him in his stroll,
left the room, having previously deposited a
book upon the table. Upon this Penguin instantly pounced, eagerly opening it, in the hope
that it might afford some clue to the real name,
profession, and pursuits, or, at all events, to
the taste of the owner. In vain did he search
eagerly for any inscription, either at the beginning or end; there was none: but, for this dis-

appointment, he was amply compensated, when, upon referring to the title-page, he found that it was an American treatise upon his favourite science of geology, illustrated with engravings. The whole truth now flashed upon him at once; the stranger was palpably a geological tourist, who meant to pass some time at Thaxted in exploring the neighbourhood, and he had no doubt that he had at that moment gone up-stairs for his hammer and wallet.

So completely did he abandon himself to this beatific vision, that when Henry returned to the parlour, he ran towards him with extended hands, exclaiming, "Aha! my young friend— for such I shall henceforth call you, close and secret as you were, have I found you out, classified you? You are a brother geologist, I see,"—and he held up the book in triumphant proof of the assertion; "and I am all anxiety to know, before we stir a step farther, or lift a hammer, whether we agree in our theories. Do you hold with Hutton or Werner? are you a Vulcanian or a Neptunian?"

A fit of coughing, brought on by the eagerness and rapidity of his utterance, as he ran on

with other questions of similar import, afforded
Henry an opportunity of disclaiming all knowledge of geology, or of the different systems to
which allusion had been made; a declaration
that only produced an incredulous smile from
Penguin, as he pointed to the book in his hand,
and exclaimed, " Here is your refutation,
young man; a proof in black and white that
f not an adept, you are at least, like myself, a
dabbler, a smatterer, an admirer of the noble
and transcendent science."

" The book was given to me in America
to be delivered to a friend of the author's in
London. I forgot the commission, and discovering it in my portmanteau, brought it down-
stairs that I might dispatch it by the coach to
ts destination. I have not even read it, for I
am no admirer of the science upon which it
treats."

" What!" shouted Penguin, with a mixed
look of amazement, indignation, and incredu-
ity, " not a geologist! not an admirer of the
magisterial science, which is alone worthy the
devotion of a human intellect! Did I under-

stand you rightly? Surely you are not an enemy to this noble study?"

"Not at all: I would prohibit nothing. Knowledge is power: power may be applied to useful purposes, and I would, therefore, prosecute the sciences, only making them subordinate to that greatest of all wisdom which teaches us how we may best and most extensively benefit our fellow-creatures. I would have men less consider in their studies what may prove advantageous to themselves, than what may be of value to others; and I would wish them to contemplate with much greater respect the ignorant clown who practises active benevolence, than the deepest and most accomplished scholar, who is too much immersed in the lore of past generations to attend to the wants and sufferings of the present; or the scientific inquirer who attaches himself so ardently to inanimate nature, that he neglects the nobler productions of the Deity, and has neither time nor sympathy to bestow upon his fellow-creatures. 'The proper study of mankind is man,' and, for my own part, I would

rather allay a single pang of anguish, than im-
mortalize myself by the most brilliant disco-
veries in science."

Penguin, feeling no interest in opinions which
seemed to him little better than fantastical reveries, had been turning over the leaves of the
geological treatise, instead of attending to the
speaker, when Henry, nothing offended at this
mark of disrespect, told him that if he wished
to read it, he would defer his intention of sending it to London, and take it with him when he
himself returned thither. By this offer he had
unintentionally found the direct road to the
heart of his companion, who eagerly accepted
it, and recollecting at the same time that he had
hitherto made little progress in fishing out the
hidden object of Henry's visit, jumped up, exclaiming, with his former look of animation and
good humour,

"Well, my young friend, what say you?
Shall we prosecute our intention of taking a
ramble together? The morning is beautiful!
I know the whole surrounding country within
walking distance; and though you are no geologist now, who knows but that I may make a

convert of you, knock down your objections
with my hammer, and finally coax your heart
into my wallet. Ha! ha!"

He brandished the tool in playful menace as
he spoke; and Henry declaring that he would
gladly accompany him, though he had no fear
of being made a proselyte to such a barren,
useless, and unproductive science, they sallied
forth together.

" Yonder large white house amid the trees,"
said the gossiping geologist to his companion,
"called Oakham Hall, belongs to Justinian
Frampton, 'Squire Frampton' as he is sometimes named, though it seems ridiculous enough
to bestow that title upon a Londoner, and a
West India proprietor, who only comes down
here in the summer season, and who, however
rich he may be in slaves and estates in Jamaica,
does not possess so much land in the neighbourhood as honest Frank Ringwood, whose family
have been always called, for many generations, the
Squires of Thaxted. Frampton himself is rather
a pompous, purse-proud fellow, who lives in great
style, feasts upon turtle and old Madeira, when
he is not visited with the gout, and seems dis-

posed to be hearty and neighbourly enough, as far as Lady Susan will let him. His wife, you must know, is a bit of blood, and not wanting in proud flesh I may add, in proof of which——Do you see how yonder stratum of flints is broken all along the side of that chalk-pit? What a convulsive wrench does this indicate! One can almost imagine that the earth in full swing must have knocked against some other planet to produce such a concussion, or that some tremendous earthquake——but, however, that is not the subject under discussion. We were considering, were we not, the probability that flint might be produced from the shells of marine animals deposited in the strata of chalk?"

"No, Sir, indeed: we were talking of Lady Susan Frampton."

"'Gadso, you 're right—perfectly right! but we were not wandering far from the subject, for I believe her heart to be somewhat of the flinty order—decidedly of the siliceous genus. Ha! ha! you'll excuse my being a bit of a wag. Well, sir, Lady Susan Frampton, as I was informed, although we had met at a

house in the neighbourhood, and been introduced to one another, declined calling upon me,
because I had been originally a shopkeeper.
Now, as I knew myself to be as good a man as
her husband, and independent of all the world,
I determined to give her a wipe; so when she
next honoured me with one of her cold, condescending bows, egad! I stared plump in her face,
gave her the cut complete, and took no notice of
her. When she found that I could be as rude and
arrogant as herself, she fancied, I suppose, that
I must have some sort of gentility about me,
for she called next day, and we have been upon
very civil terms ever since.. They have two
daughters, beautiful girls both of them, (though
I like the youngest the best,) and a coxcomb of
a son, who is in the army, and seems to have
the faults of both parents, without——Aha!
what have we here? This must be limestone—
a small specimen—wonder how it came here.
Let us see whether it contains any petrifactions.
Ah! I was not mistaken—take it home to
ascertain its specific gravity." And he popped
it into his wallet with as much delight as the
keen sportsman bags a pheasant.

A voice was now heard singing in a loud, merry tone, but with a foreign, nasal, sharp accent, when Penguin, looking in the direction of the sound, exclamed, " Yonder I see comes another part of Frampton's establishment, which I forgot to mention, though, with the exception of the younger daughter of whom I told you, he is the only lively inmate in that stately but stupid family. It is Pompey, their black ser-- vant. Some mischievous prank, at Barbadoes, occasioned the fellow to be severely whipped : his present master happened to be passing at the time of his punishment, and moved by his cries and supplications, purchased him on the spot from his unrelenting owner, intending to take him to Jamaica, and leave him on one of his estates in that island. On the voyage thither, Frampton, not having full possession of his gouty feet, tumbled overboard through a gangway that happened to be open, when Pom- pey, who swims like a fish, jumped after him, and saved his life by keeping his head above water till a boat was put out to their assistance. For this important service he was brought to

England, which of course ensures his freedom,
and promoted to the situation of a footman,
though utterly unqualified for the performance
of any other duty than that of wearing a gorgeous livery, standing occasionally behind the
carriage, and carrying the family prayer-books
to church on a Sunday. His mistress hates
him, never having forgiven, as it is shrewdly
suspected, his skill in swimming; but he has
no other enemy. Frampton likes him, so do his
fellow-servants; and indeed the whole village
are upon good terms with merry Pompey, for
as he has little or nothing to do in the house,
he employs nearly the whole of his time in promoting fun, frolic, and amusement wherever
they are to be found. He is a good mimic, not
in his voice, for that never alters, but with his
limbs, performing vaults and somersets like a
clown, acting a drunken man, or imitating the
pompous strut of Doctor Dotterel with a drollery
that is perfectly irresistible. He makes whistles,
pop-guns, and bows and arrows for the children;
sings songs to the women, or tells their fortunes;
plays gratis upon the fiddle whenever a rustic

dance is got up in a barn, and is always ready
for a prank or a freak of any sort, so that he is
equally popular with all ages."

" There seems to be an insuperable merriment even in the tone of his voice," observed
Henry ; " it is like the shrill but cheerful crow-
ing of the cock."

" Merriment ! he knows not what it is to be
either sick or sorry. Driven away by the sound
of his joyous chuckle, Care seems afraid to come
near him ; and even age itself, for his head is
grey, has silvered his woolly hair without having been able to tame or chill the boyish play-
fulness of his heart. With the ugliness he has
all the mischievous pranks of a young baboon,
and no small share of its activity."

The party thus described had by this time
approached, bursting as he came up into a
new song, accompanied with vehement and
appropriate gesticulations, and pausing every
now and then to laugh, or rather to smile,
for he uttered no sound at the moment. No
cachinnation, however, could be so joyous as that
silent smile, which, like the sun suddenly bursting from a dark cloud, illuminated in an in-

stant his whole countenance, displaying his
large white even teeth, imparting an absolute
flash to his eye, and raising up his low brow
in successive wrinkles, until the grey woolly
scalp was thrown backwards, while the entire
shining face was manifestly floating in enjoyment. The following was the snatch of negro-
song, which met the ear of Henry and his
companion as the black came up to them :—

Da sun begin from da sea to peep,
                    Buckara! buckara! cracko!
Da oberseer, him smack him whip,
                    Buckara! buckara! cracko!
From bed of reeds da nigger start,
Gog! if he don't, dey make him smart,
An' he go to da fiel' wid a hebby heart,
                    Buckara! buckara! cracko!

In da boiling-house, a'ter brekkas time,
                    Buckara! buckara! cracko!
Da oberseer up a ladder climb,
                    Buckara! buckara! cracko!
To see if da suggee boil to a crack,
When da nigger steal behind him back,
An' push him into da copper, smack!
                    Buckara! buckara! cracko!

" Gog! him nebber crack any mo' him dam
whip. Always floggee poor nigger, and say—

' What for oo no' make mo' suggee?'
Him make suggee himself in da big copper:
see how him like it. Ah, massa Pingwing,
morrow-morning!" And as he made his salu-
tation, he stood still, apparently with the intention of having a little gossip, while he
pursued his occupation of fashioning a pop-gun
out of some alder, of which he had gathered
a bough.

" Always busy in making playthings for
the children," said the geologist; " I don't
know what the young folks would do without you."

" Who ebber tink o' dat?—No, Massa
Pingwing mean what *I* do widout *em*. I lub
da little pickaninny; what for? Pompey ole
man dere, (and he pointed to the grizzled
wool upon his poll,) but Pompey got libely
lilly boy here, (patting his heart, and unsheath-
ing his teeth with a radiant smile.) Him blood
so red and so merry as ebber, and Gog! him
limbs not berry ole." With these words, he
popped the knife into his mouth, let fall the
branch of alder, threw his hands upon the
ground, and performing a rapid somerset, con-

tinued, " Aha, Massa Pingwing, what oo tink
o' dat? not berry ole, hey?"

" No, indeed, Pompey, I was just observing
that you are as lissome as a monkey, and by no
means unlike one in other respects."

" Berry true, massa, berry true, when I wear
ma fine libbery on da Sabba'-day, and go da
church ater my lady, um like Jacko monkey;
dress op fine, berry fine, and um long for da
fiddle to hab a dance. Ma blood berry full o'
dance, him dance widout a fiddle. No get libbery now, but white jacket; no like monkey
now, Massa."

" I should have thought he would have felt
flattered by the comparison," said Penguin to
Henry, " but he seems more ashamed of Mr.
Frampton's gorgeous livery than of the sable
and ugly one that Nature has given him."

Penguin did not think it necessary to lower
his voice in making this observation, which he
perhaps imagined to be above the comprehen-
sion of his black auditor. The latter, how
ever, recognizing it with a nod of the head,
and the exclamation of " Berry true!" con-
tinued--" Massa Pingwing always busy, same

as Pompey; Massa no mind break da stone, dig da earth, go down da pit, climb da cliff, work hard, and wear jacket all same as nigger, ony mine white and mo' smart like. Gog! tink it come to be da fashion; saw two gemmen die morning all da same as Massa; look at da groun berry sharp, look at da big stone, talkee talkee one anoder, and den tap! tap! break him a pieces as if him a great cocoa-nut full o' meatée."

"Hey! how! what! Pompey; two gentlemen did you say?"

"Iss, Massa; one in da brown jacket, one in da blue."

"Ha! these must be the two geologists I heard of that came over here last week, and were supposed to be from Christ-church."

"Iss, Massa; I left 'em in da cross-road to Chrishursh, under da great marl-pit."

"Ah, ha! are they poaching upon my manor? There have been some very curious things found in that pit. Shall we join them, my young friend? I dare say they have made some interesting discovery."

Henry signified a ready assent, and Pom-

pey having declared, in answer to Penguin's
enquiries, that the shortest way to the spot was
over the field to their left, and across the miller's water, which they might easily pass by
means of the stepping-stones placed for that
purpose, pursued his way, busily employed in
the completion of his pop-gun and his song,
while the geologist and his companion hurried
forwards in the direction that had been pointed
out to them.

CHAPTER IV.

" Our gayness and our guilt are all besmirch'd
With rainy marching in the painful field."

SHAKSPEARE.

AFTER having traversed a ploughed field, not
without difficulty from the heavy nature of the
soil, they reached a wild brake, overgrown with
thistles, nettles, burs, docks, and bramble bushes,
through which they had some trouble in forcing
their way.   The geologist delighted in conquer-
ing little impediments of this nature, which at
once stimulated his ardour, and established his
character for intrepid perseverance, so that volunteering to take the lead, he manfully pushed
through every obstacle, observing to his companion that a good sportsman never stood upon
trifles in following the game, and that his fustian jacket and trowsers were expressly adapted
for emergencies like the present.   His seal-skin

cap, however, was twitched off, and it was not
without a scratched face that its owner was enabled to redeem it ; while his wallet was obliged
to pay similar toll to the various briers which
it had to pass. Thus acting as a pioneer to
Henry, whose clothes were not so well calculated for the warfare in which they were engaged, they at length emerged upon the brow of a
rough descent shelving down into a little glen,
called the Run, on account of the increased
rapidity of the miller's stream, which hurried
along the bottom in its course to the sea. It was
shallow, except in heavy rains, and large stepping-stones were usually thrown into it for the
accommodation of such rustics or others as had
occasion to cross it. On arriving at the spot it
was found that these had been removed, probably by some mischievous urchin, and Penguin, who with all his geological love of the
earth and its contents, did not by any means
stand so well affected towards cold water, observed with a disappointed look, that it would take
them a mile out of their way to go round by the
mill. To this circuit he was preparing to submit, not without manifest reluctance against the

delay it would occasion, especially as the objects of his search might in the mean time have be-taken themselves to some other quarter, when he heard the faint sound of voices immediately succeeded by the click of a hammer upon some hard substance.

" Gadso !" he eagerly exclaimed, grasping his own hammer as if he longed to be at work, " there they are, there they are, sure enough ! I warrant me they are hard at it. The pit is only beyond the first field on the other side the bank. What say you, my young friend, shall we dash through this paltry runnel? It is not above knee deep, and a little sousing will not hurt either of us. ' Nothing venture, nothing have,' should be the motto of a staunch geolo-gist, and though you are not one of us, you probably swimmed across the Missisippi and the Ohio before you left America, and will therefore never boggle at such a puddle as this."

" I have no objection whatever to pass it, but my reverence to truth compels me to tell you, that you are mistaken with respect to the

Missisippi and the Ohio; and my regard for grammar obliges me to add, that the preterite of swim, is swam, swom, or swum."

" All right, perfectly right, my young Domine. Bravo! here goes: follow me, and fear nothing." So saying, Penguin sprang into the stream, intending to cross it in two or three long strides, but instead of meeting the firm footing he expected, he sank up to the knee in a sort of black quicksand, and being thrown upon his face, was obliged to scramble in the best way he could to the opposite bank, where he arrived in a most ruefully ducked and be- smirched condition. Quickly recovering himself, however, his misadventure seemed to have made him " bate no jot of heart or hope," for he began washing his swan-like legs, laughing at his own ridiculous plight, perhaps to conceal his real mortification, and expressing his surprise that his companion did not participate in his merriment.

" I never laugh at the smallest mischance or disappointment of my fellow-creatures," said Henry.

" All right, perfectly right, but I tell you beforehand, that I shall laugh most confoundedly if you are caught in the same trap."

" There would be small danger of that, even were the streamlet wider than it is." So saying he returned a little way up the bank to give himself the benefit of the descent, and then running forward at full speed, cleared the water at a single leap.

" Gadso, my young friend !" exclaimed the astonished geologist, " you vault like a roebuck, or rather like an arrow out of a boy. Did you learn this trick in America ?"

" Athletic exercises are conducive to health ; health should be our primary consideration, and I have therefore diligently practised every sport that might contribute to strength or agility, until I have obtained a command over my limbs, which I consider preferable to a knowledge of all the languages upon earth. There is both pleasure and utility in having the full possession of my own body, while there is neither the one nor the other in wasting time upon the acquisition of a foreign tongue, for the English language embodies within itself, either in

its native stores or by means of translation, all
the wisdom that the world has ever known."

"All right, Domine, all right: I must needs
confess, that your gymnastic exercises are better
than all Latin and Greek ones in the world for
carrying a fellow clean and dry over a treacher-
ous brook like this cursed Miller's-run. Gadso!
I haven't lost my hammer, have I? No, here it
is, all safe."

In the triumph of the moment he twirl'd it
high up in the air, again catching it adroitly by
the handle, and his abstersions being now completed, so far as the sable stains could be ef-
faced, he again hurried forward to intercept
his brother geologists. After climbing up the
opposite bank, and again descending, they
crossed the field to which Penguin had alluded,
and making their way into the cross-road,
presently reached the bottom of an extensive
marl-pit, of which the precipitous summit was
tufted with alder and other bushes. Penguin
listened eagerly for the sound of voices or
implements, and gazed round in vain for the
expected men of science: he could only perceive a couple of labourers sitting in the shade

and quietly dispatching their bread and cheese,
while a dog, who had the charge of their hats
and a little flask of beer, saluted the strangers
with a bristling mane, and an angry growl.
" Ah! lame Richard, how are you? how are
you, Joe Penfold?" said the geologist, who
knew every individual rustic and pauper for
miles round—"which way are the two gentlemen gone who were here just now, making
mineralogical researches?"

In answer to this inquiry, the men declared
that they had not seen a soul in the course of
the morning, except Squire Frampton's black-
a-moor, who intended crossing the field to the
Miller's-run, until they told him the stepping-
stones had been removed, which induced him
to go round by the road.—" What! were there
not two gentlemen upon the spot? there must
have been—I heard their hammers not ten
minutes ago."

" Lord love ye! that was we;—we was a
cracking flints for the rooad when the black
chap came up to us."

" And one of them wears a brown and the
other a blue jacket," observed Henry.

A blank chop-fallen look attested Penguin's conviction that he had been bamboozled by the Negro, and the angry blood quickly rushed to his features as he exclaimed—"Curse that impudent black fellow! then I have been regularly hoaxed; these were the gentlemen geologists who were breaking stones, and I have scrambled through thorns and thistles, and have been soused in the mud and dirty water of the Miller's-run all for nothing."

"Iss, Massa, iss," cried a cackling voice from above, and upon looking upwards they beheld the white teeth, and black, shining, smiling face of Pompey, protruded from the overhanging alders which had just supplied him with a new pop-gun.

"Massa Pinwing say um look like a monkey : aha! what oo look like ooseff, wid oo black legs and oo souse jacket? Better um look like a monkey nor an ass."

" This impertinence, fellow, shall be made known to your master," cried the geologist.

" Gog! berry like, cause Pompey tell um himseff, dat a may hab da fuss laugh."

This observation probably suggested to

Penguin, that as he could gain nothing by his wrath, he had better view the whole affair as a joke, for replacing his uplifted hammer in his wallet, he said with a forced smile—" After all it was not a bad hoax, and I might well have expected it, knowing the black fellow to have as many tricks as a baboon. It must be confessed, that he has made a precious fool of me."

" Iss, Massa, iss, berry true," cried Pompey disclosing his white teeth with a broad radiant smile ; and being now apparently satisfied with the triumph he had obtained, he quitted the overhanging boughs, and pursued his way along the uplands, shouting at the top of his voice—

—" Da nigger steal behind him back,
And push him into da copper, smack !
Buckara ! buckara ! cracko !"

The two labourers in the marl-pit, although Penguin had to a certain extent conciliated their good wishes by wearing a jacket no better than their own, and by often chattering familiarly with them, as he did indeed with all the world, had still such a poor opinion of his intellects, from his volunteering the drudgery of breaking

stones, when, if he chose, he might sit at home,
and swill strong ale all day long, that their looks
and tone of voice in conversing with him generally betrayed the same compassionate kind of
contempt that they would have assumed had
they been addressing the parish idiot. Upon
the present occasion they had at first observed a
certain degree of respect, but when they comprehended the full extent of Pompey's trick,
when they understood that they themselves had
been palmed off upon Penguin for gentlemen,
and that in his eagerness to share their society,
he had floundered through the mud and water
of the Miller's-run, as his bedraggled plight
ludicrously attested, all the barriers of respect
were broken down, and they both burst into a
horse laugh, loud enough to send dissonant
echoes from the sides of the pit, and to be answered by a distant *Da Capo* of Pompey's song
as he was retreating homewards. Penguin had
no alternative but to join them, which he did
with an assumed hilarity, and then turning to
Henry with a somewhat sardonic expression,
exclaimed:—" You are the only grave fellow
among us, my young friend; why don't you

laugh? Gadso, it's a capital joke, and I really enjoy it myself: why don't you laugh?"

"I told you before, that I never laughed at the smallest misadventure of a fellow-creature, and you must allow me to observe, that you have brought this trouble upon yourself by comparing Pompey, in his own hearing, to a monkey. His retaliation is a moderate one, though no retaliation can be excusable, since two wrongs will never make one right. It is unjustifiable in principle, and may be dangerous in practice, ever to wound the feelings of another, even in jest; for as retorts and revenges generally double or quadruple in severity the last offence given, that which began in mirth may quickly end in murder."

"All right, my young Domine, perfectly right. Gad! one may learn more by listening to you than to one of Dr. Dottrel's sermons, though that, perhaps, is no great compliment. Come, shall we pursue our ramble? I don't value my sousing a single button. It's vastly pleasant, isn't it?"

With these words, he walked away at a brisk pace, by no means sorry, as it seemed, to escape

from the boisterous merriment and ridiculing
looks of the labourers, whom he quitted without his usual valedictory notice, and the click
of whose hammers, as they again plied their
work, fell upon his ear with a much less grateful and stimulating effect than when he had
previously heard the same sound. Had Henry
been what is called a wag, he would not have
failed to draw his companion's attention to it,
and to banter him upon the renewed labours of
the gentlemen geologists; but this was foreign
to his nature. His benevolence was so sensitive
and delicate, his sympathy with his fellow-creatures so intense, that he never indulged in any
raillery in the remotest degree calculated to
give pain. Penguin, however, was fidgetting
under the manifest apprehension of his malicious pleasantry, for he walked rapidly forwards, although it was up hill, in order to get
beyond the sinister sound of the hammers, and
talked incessantly that his companion might
not have an opportunity for venting either banter or sarcasm. " Aha! my young friend," he
briskly exclaimed, stopping to take a moment's
breath, when they had gained the summit of the

ascent ; " there 's a prospect for you ! what say
you to that ?   Is it not noble, yonder fine
stretch of wood that forms the commencement
of the New Forest, and shows us many a stout
oak destined, perhaps, to form one of our first-
rate ships, and carry the British thunder to the
remotest corners of the world ?"

" I see an open, rich, and finely-cultivated
tract that, while it smiles in beauty, promises to
yield sustenance and plenty to mankind ; and
which I consequently admire much more than
a gloomy forest, whether it be reserved for the
useless and cruel warfare of the chace, or applied to the still more hateful and guilty hos-
tilities which we may carry on against distant
nations."

" Ah ! I forgot, you have been in America,
come from the back settlements, and have had
a surfeit of trees, of which you doubtless like
the sight as little as a grocer does the taste of
figs.   I fear we shall find little to please you
in England.   You have been accustomed to a
new country, and it is natural therefore that
you should not like an old one." .

" You are widely mistaken.   In my opinion,

the inhabitants of an old country have innu-
merable advantages. They have the benefit of
every past age—for all the previous generations
of mankind may be considered as their slaves,
who, for the enjoyment of the existing race, have
made and perfected the public roads, dug wells
and canals, rendered rivers navigable, drained
morasses, fertilized the soil, beautified the surface of the country, and covered it with costly
edifices of public utility, or for private residence. It must be an additional pleasure to
the dwellers in such a country, that they may
justly consider it their home, since it contains the
bones of their forefathers; while all the monu-
ments of art, and much of the natural scenery,
being associated with the national records, are
lifted out of their mere materiality, and become
endearing and ennobling memorials; which may
usefully stimulate the people who live among
them to maintain the greatness that has been
transmitted to them. Unless, as I have done,
you had witnessed the formation of a new settlement in a new country, you could hardly
imagine how grievously the want of all this,
how deeply the total absence of an antiquity is

felt and regretted,—how disheartening it is to begin with felling trees, making roads, digging wells, and performing the most severe and servile drudgery long before you can even attempt to raise a crop ; how strange and uninteresting is the dumb scenery which can tell us nothing of our ancestors or of the past ages, though it may painfully remind us that it has been the haunt of savages and wild beasts ;—how oppressive is the misgiving, when he who toils reflects that he may perchance perish before he has conquered the stubborn earth, or that, after all, he may be only slaving, like the bee, to raise honey for strangers."

" More fool he ! Why can't such fellows remain where they were born ?"

" Because it is better to have the hope of living in a new country than the fear of starving in an old one: over-population and want drive many to the necessity of colonizing ; but a still greater number, and of a better class, have sometimes fled to the woods and wilds to enjoy that paramount moral good which more than compensates for all the physical disadvantages of a new settlement."

" Ay, ay ! what may that be ?"

" Civil and religious liberty ; equal rights, and uncorrupt institutions, seldom to be found in an old country, where time, that rots every thing, does not even spare the bulwarks of freedom and justice, and where the very progress of civilization and luxury works the greatest perversion and abuse in those establishments which were originally the most pure and wholesome. The combined advantages of the past and the present are, perhaps, most likely to be found in an old country which has recently purged and regenerated itself by a revolution ; for the moral as well as the natural soil is best fertilized by the ashes of the destroyed rankness, corruption, and overgrowth which itself had thrown up."

" Why, my young friend, what the deuce do you call yourself !—a jacobin, a radical, a revolutionist? Gadso! it's lucky Doctor Dotterel does not hear you, or you would be excommunicated, anathematised. Come, come, I understand nothing of these matters, let us talk of something rational. Do you see those men at work, digging the foundations of a

house? They turned up last week what I considered a specimen of valuable ore, and the
owner of the ground, poor fellow! thought
he was going to make his fortune all in
a hurry; but, egad! it proved to be only a
species of mica, or Glimmer, as the workmen
call it, or something of that sort, and the churl
threw it at my head, when he found I had elated
him with false hopes.—Aha! what have we
here? I must give this ferruginous clod a touch
of my hammer, it has a shrewdly mineral aspect. You see, I literally leave no stone un-
turned to succeed in my objects; and, indeed,
I may well keep a sharp look out, for it was
not far from here that, about a month ago, I
stumbled upon a foliaceous, or flaky substance,
that had very much the appearance of talc.
I'll tell you the whole history of my finding it,
which is really interesting,—but, egad! I forgot, you are no geologist; and though Shakspeare, you know, says that there are sermons in
stones, you have little inclination, I dare say,
to hear sermons on stones. Now, between these
trees, we can just catch a peep at the old-fashioned towers and pointed gables of the Manor-

house, where——Gadso! I protest I had nearly
forgotten all about it."

In the multiplicity of objects which successively claimed Penguin's attention, one was very
apt to push its predecessor out of his head, a
process which had taken place more than once
this morning since he had started from the
George. The sight of the Manor-house, re-
calling to his recollection the surmise of Tony,
as to the object of Henry's visit, reminded him
at the same time that he had hitherto made no
progress towards discovering it; and being now
disposed to attach more importance to the
ostler's assertion than he had yielded to it at
the time, he proceeded without delay to sound
his companion upon the subject. "Yonder old
building is the residence of his worship Mr.
Gideon Welbeck, one of our justices of the
peace. Do you know any thing of him?"

Henry answered in the negative.

"No great loss," continued his companion.
"He is a strange creature and by no means
popular in the county. His legal knowledge,
however, is of use to him as a magistrate, the
duties of which office he discharges with such

zeal, vigilance, and impartiality, that his brother justices, too indolent or too ignorant to
assist or compete with him, voluntarily abandon to him all the troublesome and executive
business of the district.   I told you that he was
generally disliked; but, if all be true that I have
heard, he is rather an object of compassion
than hatred, for—stop! stay! look at this bit of
slate, do you observe how the dark veins that
cross it are broken and continued again half an
inch lower, manifestly proving that it has once
been in a liquid state.   There's another bit,
which I must pop into my wallet.—Gadso! let
me see, where was I; were we not talking of
the vertical strata which Werner— ?"

" No, Sir, you were remarking that Mr.
Welbeck was rather an object of compassion
than—"

" All right—perfectly right, so I was, and
so he is, if all be true that is rumoured; for
the poor man, such I may well call him, in
spite of his riches, has an only son, who, after
taking to gambling, and all sorts of dissolute
courses, by which he was perpetually torment-
ing his father in the most sensitive part—that is

to say, in his pocket, completed his own ruin and degradation by marrying a low woman of infamous character. Upon this occasion old Welbeck, who is a man of violent passions, solemnly cursed his son, struck him out of his will, and swore that he would never forgive his daughter, or any one else, who should ever mention his name in his presence. It has been even whispered that the son was subsequently guilty of forgery, for he fled to the continent with his disreputable wife, and has never been heard of since. Egad! talking of his daughter, puts me in mind that Tony, of the George, told me you were acquainted with Miss Welbeck— is it so? How comes it? She rarely leaves home?"

"We lately passed a few days in the same boarding-house at Southampton, where she went to visit an aunt, and I confess that I was much struck by the timid gentleness of her manners, and the resignation with which she seemed to submit to some deep-rooted melancholy."

"Aha! my young friend, have I found you out? So this, then, was the object of your visit to Thaxted."

" You are quite mistaken ; it was not until I arrived at Thaxted, that I recollected that her father resided in its vicinity."

" Indeed !" exclaimed the geologist, casting an incredulous look at his companion's coun- tenance, where, however, he beheld such legible evidences of sincerity and truth, that he could not doubt his assertion, and being now reduced to a non-plus, he determined to satisfy his curiosity by the point-blank question of— " Pray, then, may I inquire what *was* the object of your coming hither ?"

" I come for the purpose of visiting a gen- tleman in this neighbourhood upon some affairs of business."

" A gentleman in this neighbourhood !—I know them all—I will introduce you to him. What is his name ? "

" Mark Penguin," said Henry.

" Mark Penguin !" reiterated the geologist, with an expression of amazement, not altogether unmingled with alarm, and then endeavouring to recover himself and appear unconcerned, he added, " What can you have to say to *him* ?" Taken as he was by surprise, he had still pre-

sence of mind enough to resolve on preserving
his incognito till this point should be cleared up,
for he was not without apprehension that the
ghost of some old smuggling transaction might
rise up in judgment against him, though it appeared utterly inexplicable how this young man,
but just arrived from America, where he had
passed nearly all his life, should have become
implicated with him and his former contraband
practices.   Loquacious as he was, he preserved
a cautious silence, and gazed with an eager,
reddened face upon Henry, as the latter proceeded to state that the first husband of Captain
Tenby's widow, had been a Mr. Joseph Penguin, of Montreal, brother to Mr. Mark Penguin, lately resident at Southampton, to whom
the widow wished to deliver certain papers and
documents left by her deceased first husband,
as well as to pay her personal respects to so
near a relative, and one with whom she had formerly been in habit of frequent correspondence.
In point of fact, Mark had received a letter
from her some years before, announcing the
death of her husband, in circumstances that
scarcely promised to leave her a maintenance ;

but as Penguin, like most other worldly men, had an instinctive horror of poor relations, he never noticed her communication, justifying himself at the time by the reflection, that as she was an American, she ought to look for support from her connexions in that country, and vindicating his subsequent silence by choosing to take it for granted, that if she had need of his assistance, she would have made farther application to him. This she would probably have done, but that her marriage with Captain Tenby rendered such a step unnecessary, and in her pique at his leaving her first letter unanswered, she had suffered the correspondence to drop altogether, though she had now become eager to renew the acquaintance, upon learning that her kinsman had retired from business with a handsome fortune. Penguin was by no means pleased with Henry's communication at the first blush of the affair. Conscious, perhaps, that his character did not merit any extraordinary homage, he always suspected the motives of those who said they came to pay their respects to him, and as he set down the averment about the papers and documents for a mere pre-

text, he concluded that the object of the widow's
visit to Europe was to make a vehement appeal
to his feelings and his purse. The vision of a
weeping female in weeds, a white cambric hand-
kerchief in her hand, her heart full, and her
pocket empty, began to float before his imagination, and he determined not to disclose himself until he had ascertained the probability of
his being haunted with any such apparition.
The subsequent information that he received,
soon dissipated all his apprehensions, whether
pathetic or pecuniary. So little importance did
Henry attach to money, and so small an income
appeared to him a competency, that without
mentioning the exchange he had voluntarily
made with the widow, he stated the amount of
her fortune, adding that he himself, owing to
the bounty of the captain, who had adopted him
as his son, was in independent circumstances,
and that the necessary transferring of stock, consequent upon his coming of age, which had been
the cause of their voyage to England, had just
been completed in London.

This unexpected intelligence effected an in-
stantaneous and surprising change in the mind

of Penguin. Attaching a much more important meaning to the words " independent circumstances" than Henry had intended to convey, he saw at once the propriety of cultivating
a strict intimacy with a sister-in-law who had a
comfortable provision for life, and a young man
of fortune, by connecting himself with whom he
might materially increase his own consequence
and the opinion of his gentility in the neighbourhood. Such anticipations had rapidly flitted through his head, while his companion had
been speaking, and he had no sooner concluded,
than he burst into a forced laugh, exclaiming,
" Gad! I was determined to surprise you—did
I not keep my incognito famously ? Whom do
you think you have been talking to all this
while ? why, to no other than the very man of
whom you are in search, to Mark Penguin
himself, and most happy am I, my dear young
friend, to make your acquaintance; since, as
you must indeed have observed, I took a strange
fancy to you from the very first moment I beheld you."

Here he seized his companion's hand, and
shaking it with a heartiness which might now

be pronounced genuine, since his disposition was really cordial, when unchecked by any fears of a pecuniary nature, he expressed his delight at their happy meeting, inquired very particularly after Mrs. Tenby's health, and protested that he would not part with his companion, now that they had so fortunately encountered, but that he must go home and dine with him, that they might arrange their future plans and proceedings. "My forlorn plight," said he, looking down at his bedraggled clothes, "hardly qualifies me for prolonging our ramble, which we will, however, resume to-morrow; and, to tell you the truth, I find myself so much chilled by the mud and water of that cursed Miller's-run, that I shall not be sorry to change my soiled equipments for clean and dry garments. The geologists, however, ought not to quarrel with the earth for leaving its honourable mark upon us:—We are of the earth—earthy. Ha, ha! you'll excuse my being a bit of a wag. Come along, my young friend, come along."

Henry signified his willing acceptance of the invitation, and Penguin accordingly proceeded at an accelerated pace towards his own dwelling.

CHAPTER V.

The way is plain before us—there is now
The lover's visit first, and then the vow
Mutual and fond, the marriage-rite—the bride
Brought to her home with all a husband's pride.
But in short time he saw with much surprise
Commanding frowns, and anger-darting eyes. .

Crabbe.

THEY who are young should not marry yet, those who are old should not marry at all, says Thales the philosopher. In his prudence and worldly wisdom, Penguin had observed the first clause of the apopthegm; but when his independent circumstances authorized him, as he thought, to follow his own fancy, he had neglected the last half of the position. Just as he was meditating a retirement from business, he

was seized with a tedious malady, for which
change of air was prescribed; and he accordingly engaged lodgings, at the distance of a few
miles from Southampton, in the house of a widow named Jarvis, apparently a very respectable woman, who, with her daughter, promised
to take all possible care of the invalid, and to
make him quite as comfortable as if he were at
home. The mother, an exceedingly plausible,
but shrewd and artful woman of the world, no
sooner learned the circumstances of her lodger,
than she felt a deep interest in performing this
promise, having promptly formed a hope that,
by proper management, she might entrap him
as a husband for her daughter. Laura, for
such was the name of the latter, was a fine,
showy-looking girl, somewhat more dashing in
her style of dress than became her station,
though by no means an unattractive figure,
especially to a bachelor verging upon sixty.
No sooner was she apprized of her mother's designs, than she entered into them with the utmost alacrity, and prosecuted them with a pro-
portionate address. Rendering her appearance
as alluring as possible, she found an excuse, in

the invalid's state of health, for being perpetually about his person, preparing with her own hand his slops and broths, administering his medicaments, providing his little delicacies when he became convalescent, and omitting no opportunity of amusing his mind, while she contributed to alleviate his personal ailments.

Penguin was neither ungrateful for her unremitting attentions, nor insensible to the influence of her personal charms; but as she was more than young enough to be his daughter, her appearance rather suggested to him the propriety of his choosing a wife with similar qualifications, but of a more appropriate age, than presented her to his mind as calculated to supply the desiderated helpmate in her own person. In fact, he had no idea that she would accept a husband so much older than herself, even were he bold enough to overlook the disparity of their years, and make her an offer of his hand; in which persuasion he prepared to leave the house, not, however, without warm expressions and liberal testimonies of his gratitude. Alarmed at these demonstrations of departure, Mrs. Jarvis proceeded to adopt such effectual mea-

sures for the attainment of her object, and was
so artfully and effectually seconded by her
daughter, that in the course of a few weeks
Laura became Mrs. Penguin.

In explanation of the young lady's anxiety
to effect this incongruous union, it may be
stated that she had, a year or two before this
period, been so unfortunate as to commit a *faux
pas*, which, by the mother's wary management, had been carefully hushed up at the moment; but as it was by no means impossible
that the affair might transpire, an event which
would not tend to increase the number of can-
didates for her hand, she deemed it highly advisable to get married with as little delay as
possible.   Mrs. Jarvis was the more anxious to
see her settled, from her knowledge of Laura's
light, unsteady character; and when to these
weighty considerations were added a present
settlement of two hundred pounds a-year, and
the prospect of becoming a well provided widow,
should she survive Penguin, of which there
could be little doubt, disparity of years appeared so trivial an objection, as scarcely to
deserve a moment's thought.   In the daughter's

estimation, indeed, the advanced age of her
husband was rather an advantage, as bringing
within nearer view that happy period when she
might indemnify herself at the altar of love, for
those sacrifices which she now made at the
shrines of wealth and prudence.

To judge by external manifestations, never
was so watchful, so diligent, so anxious a wife.
She took into her own hands the complete control of his household, the superintendence of
his health, the direction of almost every action
of his life, so that her love, for such her husband chose to call it, soon degenerated into
an absolute tyranny, which she sometimes exercised in a way rather painful to his feelings,
by displaying her authority in the presence of
his friends and visitants. To reconcile himself
and others to this obtrusive domination, he
would candidly confess that her fondness became occasionally importunate and troublesome,
but that knowing how she doated upon him,
how deep and tender was her solicitude for his
welfare, he must be the most ungrateful of men,
in fact, little better than a brute, did he not
humour her in these little, affectionate, though

perhaps over-anxious interferences. Now and
then he would vary the ground he took in de-
fence of his own independence, pointing out beforehand this foible in his better half, declaring
that there was nothing in which he took so
much delight, after geology, as in the display
of character, and volunteering to *draw out* Mrs.
Penguin's foibles and peculiarities in justification of his assertions; a process by which he
flattered himself that he should keep the upper
hand in the opinion of his guests at the very
moment that he most submissively yielded himself up to the lady's dominion.

Seeing her stand at the open door of the
house as he approached, he gave Henry a hasty
intimation of these particulars, as if to prepare
him for an effusion of her petulant fondness,
notwithstanding which caution, his companion
was somewhat surprised at the shrewish tone of
reprehension in which she exclaimed, as soon as
she had discovered her husband's bespattered
condition, " Hoity-toity! Mr. P. is this a
plight for a gentleman to come home in, splashed and draggled as if he were a common hedger
and ditcher, who had been dragging a fish-

pond, or cleaning out a cesspool? What! have
you been diving after stones into the mud and
water, like a Newfoundland dog? Faugh! it
must have been some filthy place, for it has the
noisomest smell I ever came nigh. You'll be
drowned or smothered one of these days, if you
go on with such foolish dangerous freaks, pok-
ing into wells, and grubbing into pits, after
rubbish and old brickbats."

"After minerals, spars, and subterranean rari-
ties, you mean. Zooks! my dear, it would never
do for a staunch geologist like me to boggle at
every puddle or quagmire,"—and he winked his
eye at Henry as he spoke, as if to intimate that
he enjoyed the voluble anxiety of his spouse.

"I 'm no person to be winked at, nor is it a
matter to be passed off with a nod, Mr. P.,"
resumed the magisterial dame; "when you may
be laid up again for six weeks with a rheumatic
attack, as you were with a sprained ankle, after
tumbling down the cliff of Christchurch Bay,
in ferreting out an old bone."

"An elephant's tooth, a rare and invaluable
fossil, as I hope to be saved!" said the geologist, appealing to Henry. "That was the

pleasantest roll I ever had, for I kept the elephant's tooth in my hand all the while."

"Yes; but you had one of your own knocked out of your head, which is little better than a fool's exchange; and I found nothing so pleasant in having to nurse you early and late, night and day, and you as cross all the time as two sticks."

"Gadso! I believe I must plead guilty to that charge, though I had the best nurse in all the world. But I cannot bear to be tied by the leg; it 's like caging an eagle."

"Cooping a goose, you mean, Mr. P., and cooped you are again likely to be, if you stand talking any longer in your wet clothes; so be pleased to change them as fast as you can. Your things have been airing ever since breakfast-time, and you will find them all ready in your room; for somehow or other, I had a misgiving that you would come home as if you had been dragged through a horse-pond. I 'm sure it 's a mercy you have one like me to think for ye, and look after ye, and take care of ye."

"'Gad! there 's some truth in that," whispered Penguin to his companion, as he led him

forwards into the house: "faithful, fond creature—admirable manager—truly attached to
me—invaluable wife, to be sure! Did you see
how I drew her out, on purpose to exhibit the
little oddities of her character to you? play'd
her off famously, didn't I? That's the way I
always serve her. Vastly amusing sometimes."

By this time they had reached a handsome
parlour, when the geologist, having retired to
his toilet, Henry had an opportunity of observing that the room bespoke the taste of its
owner, being decorated with engravings of minerals, petrifactions, shells, corals, and various
vegetable and animal fossils, while the mantel-
piece was encumbered with specimens of the
same nature, all neatly ticketed and labelled,
in Penguin's own round legible hand-writing.
Only a short interval had elapsed, when the
geologist, who was rapid in all his movements,
re-entered the apartment, so much improved in
his appearance, that Henry could hardly recognize in the really respectable-looking figure now
before him, his late companion of the shabby
fustian jacket, seal-skin cap, and loaded wallet.
Penguin, however, had by no means changed

his habits with his habiliments; for observing
that his guest had been examining, for want of
better occupation, one of the fossils, he immediately exclaimed, "Aha! my' young friend,
that's a rarity, is it not? But these are nothing; only the dunnage of my cargo, as I may
say. Come along, come along to my museum,
and you shall see all my treasures." So saying,
he seized the arm of his victim, and hurried
him, *nolens volens,* to the room in question;
a spacious apartment, surrounded with glazed
mahogany-cases, well filled with geological curi-
osities, mineral and fossil, all bearing inscriptions and numbers, to enable their proprietor to
refer them to their proper species and classes.

Being now upon his own dunghill, no cock
who had found a pearl could crow more loudly
and lustily; and although Henry might have
truly exclaimed, " *Non sum Gallus, ideoquè
non reperi gemmam,*" he submitted to the infliction without a single symptom of impatience;
for, however his manners might occasionally de-
viate from conventional forms and observances,
he was never deficient in that truest and best of
all politeness which has its source in benevo-

ence. No sooner, therefore, did he perceive the
unfeigned delight with which Penguin rode his
harmless hobby, than he gave him his entire attention, more for the purpose of gratifying his
host, than from any interest that he took in the
display of his treasures. He even courteously
assisted in referring to sundry engravings and
scientific books upon a large table in the centre,
of the room, when illustrations or descriptions
were required of any particular specimens, a
process which was facilitated by labels pasted
upon the bottom of each by Penguin's own
hand.

It was however no small gratification to Henry,
especially as he had acquired an importunate
appetite by his excursion, when he was relieved
from this duty by the announcement of dinner,
and ushered to a board spread with a copious-
ness which he had hardly anticipated. Mrs.
Penguin was none of those lenten housewives
who could be taken by surprise. She never had
occasion to excuse a shabby dinner to an unexpected guest, by saying she wished he had
given her notice of his coming; nor to an invited one, by the doubtful compliment of telling

him she had treated him as a friend. With the
common mistake of under-bred people, she considered expensive clothes, and the maintenance
of a handsome table, the distinguishing and in-
fallible characteristics of gentility; and being at
once vain of her person, and somewhat over,
addicted to good living, she never failed to
bedizen herself every day with bustling and
exuberant finery, and to sit down to a very
substantial and diversified dinner. During the
progress of the repast, Mrs. Penguin, whose
zeal for her husband's health was of a most
fidgetty and fussy character, performed for him
the same unwelcome office discharged by Sancho
Panza's physician, laying an authoritative in-
terdict upon all such viands as she thought
calculated to disagree with him. Upon the
present occasion, he would gladly have dis-
pensed with her tyrannical veto, more especially
as she herself spared none of the forbidden
dishes; but she was neither disposed to relax
in her vigilance, nor even to relent at his
occasional appeals, to which she generally replied by a peevish—" Pooh! pooh! don't tell
me, Mr. P. don't you remember how ill it

made you at such and such a time?" always
taking care to specify the exact day. At the
same moment she generally ordered the servant
to bring from the sideboard and to place before
him some little delicacy of which she knew him
to be particularly fond, and it was by this sort
of double solicitude, thwarting his palate when
it could not be safely gratified, and indulging
it where his health did not forbid, that she
had established and maintained her ascendency.
Penguin never opposed her officious dictation,
but as he felt it to be somewhat derogatory, he
again seized the opportunity of whispering
to his guest, as soon as her back was turned,
" Haven't I played upon her foibles finely!
I didn't want any of those dishes—never touch
them, but resolved to let you see what a sharp
look-out she keeps upon my health ; what 's the
consequence ? Never ill; neither sick nor sorry
—don't spend five guineas a year upon apothe-
caries and doctors; all owing to her, excellent
creature! devotedly attached to me, invaluable
wife! It's really too bad of me, but I 'm so
fond of exhibiting character, that I purposely
humour her now and then, just to draw out

those little distinctive traits, those amiable peculiarities that I mentioned. Described her well,
didn't I, hey ?"

Notwithstanding her prodigious merits as a
wife, and his own skill in exhibiting them, her
absence evidently freed him from a certain degree of awkwardness and restraint; for he now
talked with a more cheerful volubility, severely
scolded the man servant who brought in the
wine, not so much for the alleged shaking of
the basket, which was indeed an imaginary
offence, as to prove that he could at least exercise proper authority over his domestics; ex-
tolled his claret, smacked his lips, pushed about
the bottle, disserted rather pompously upon his
fortune, his museum, and the respectable and
wealthy neighbours who visited him; and having thus, as he thought, re-established that
dignity which might perchance have been lower-
ed, in the eyes of his guest, by the domination
exercised by Mrs. Penguin, his ruling passion
of curiosity recovered its sway, and he proceeded to interrogate his companion as to his
plans, prospects, and intentions. Henry, who
was upon all occasions frank and open as the

day, stated that his mother designed paying a
visit to her kinsman, as soon as she had learned
his address, and obtained his permission for
doing so, which had been the object of his own
visit to Thaxted; and that he himself, purport-
ing to settle in England, should probably fix
wherever his mother did, being perfectly indifferent as to localities. The last statement was
by no means unacceptable to Penguin, who, in
the desire of relieving the occasional tedium of
his life, and in the belief that he should increase
his respectability by promoting an intimacy with
Henry, whom he set down for a young man of
handsome fortune, was already anxious to secure him as a permanent neighbour, an object
most likely to be attained by inviting him to
become his temporary guest. Such an important step, however, was not to be hazarded without the previous concurrence of his wife, whom
he forthwith sought, assigning as the sole motive of his proposed arrangement the desire of
contributing to her comfort by the society of
Mrs. Tenby. Mrs. Penguin, who had been
much struck by Henry's handsome appearance
and frank manners, giving a ready assent to his

scheme, the geologist, having now plenary authority to act, returned to the dining-room, and
after setting forth the peculiar recommendations
of his own vicinity, as a place of residence, its
salubrity, its rural beauty, its propinquity to
the sea, and above all, the great advantage of
his being able to introduce them to the best
society in the neighbourhood, he concluded with
inviting Henry and his mother to pass two or
three months with him at Grotto-house, for
such was the name of his mansion; observing, that they could thus form an opinion of the
country, and decide whether they should choose
it as a place of permanent abode. Unable to
resist, even at the expense of truth, a little bra-
vado in support of his marital authority, he
added, that he had not communicated his intention to Mrs. Penguin, that it was altogether
unnecessary, since he had only to signify his
own wishes upon any subject whatever, to en-
sure her immediate acquiescence, an observation
which he gave with a considerable air of self-
importance. Henry thankfully accepted the
invitation, adding his persuasion that his mother
would be equally glad to avail herself of her

kinsman's kindness; which point being settled, and a bottle of excellent claret having been finished, he prepared to return to his inn, in spite of the pressing instances of his host, that he should make Grotto-house his present quarters.

"I wish to see a little more of the neighbourhood," was his reply. "I told the waiter at the George, that I should pass a few days at the inn, and I never forfeit my word, unless from necessity."

"All right, perfectly right, my young Domine; but a loose promise of this sort—"

"I know not the meaning of the term;—if a promise implies performance, it cannot be loose; if it do not, it is no promise. There are no degrees of comparison in truth."

"Gadso! my young friend, you are logical; but surely you may mean what you promise, and yet be subsequently prevented from performing it."

"If the prevention be absolute it is a sufficient excuse, but mere change of will is a poor apology for breaking our word. If we violate truth in trifles, we shall soon cease to respect it

in matters of moment. You must allow me to
wish you a good evening, but I shall be at
your service to-morrow for the renewal of our
ramble."

" Well, well, I see by your peremptory look
that you have made up your mind; and since,
as they say, one man may lead a horse to the
pond, but twenty can't make him drink, you
must e'en have your own way. But you cannot think of walking, it is too far after your
long morning's ramble; and my man—a very
steady fellow is James—shall drive you over in
the gig."

" I am obliged to you, but I never ride
when I can use my own feet. All persons in
good health should use exercise; I have no
complaint, and it is fit, therefore, that I should
walk."

" Nay, if you bring your first and third into
the same denomination, and prove it by the rule
of three, there's no gainsaying you; but you
must at least allow me to accompany you part
of the way. James, bring me my hat and stick.
Shall I take my wallet and hammer? No, it
will be getting too late, and besides, we shall

renew our researches early in the morning.
Gad! though I cannot vault over the Miller's-
run like a roebuck, I can stir about upon my
legs as well as any man of my standing in the
whole county, so come along, my young friend,
come along."

So saying, he bustled at a brisk pace towards
the hall-door, where, however, he was interrupted
by the ever-watchful Mrs. Penguin, who exclaimed as he approached—" Here's doings Mr. P.!—
here's fine doings! going out again such a damp
afternoon as this, after you have been already
drenched and soused like a blind puppy; and
never thinking of those that have got to nurse
and wait upon you, should you catch cold, as
ten to one you will, or be laid up again with
the rheumatism. I have half a mind to say
you sha'n't stir a step, but if you must needs
go a gadding, when you ought to be sitting
at home and drinking a treacle-posset, let
James, at least, fasten on your gaiters, and take
this umbrella with you, and put this handker-
chief in your pocket to wrap round your throat
as you return, and don't make it late. I won't
have you be late, for it looks very like rain,

and God knows what might be the consequences of the wet and the night air, after
being be-draggled and horseponded as you have
been this morning!"

"All right, perfectly right, my dear," said
the obedient husband, putting on the gaiters
which the careful wife had brought with her.
"Gadso! there's no harm in being on the safe
side."

James in the meanwhile kept holding open
the hall-door, and surveying the process as
his master buttoned his gaiters; when Penguin,
who wanted a set-off against his own submis-
siveness to his spouse, cried with an authoritative voice and look, "Why do you stand
gaping there, you stupid fellow? get along with
you, get along!"

The man, a quiet civil rustic in a flaming
livery, withdrew without saying a word, and
Penguin, carefully accoutred for his afternoon's
walk, was at length allowed the liberty of
quitting his own house. "This good creature," he said, as they passed into the garden, " is ever on the watch for my health and
comfort. Coming in or going out, as you have

seen, she is always thinking of me: though, to be sure, I have rather led her to exhibit herself to-day for your amusement. I longed to show you her weak side. Some people would be offended at her little importunities, but that's not the case with me. Thank God! I'm not a bad husband, and with such a treasure of a wife, I should indeed be a brute if I were."

The principal object of the geologist in offering to walk part of the way back with his visitant, was to show him a grotto at the extremity of his grounds, from which his mansion had derived its name ; though, as far as shells, spars, and minerals were concerned, the dwelling-house deserved the appellation quite as much as its appendage. Here Henry underwent a fresh infliction of hard words, but the catalogue being at length completed, they pursued their way together towards Thaxted.

As they had dined early, it was yet the broad daylight of a fine summer evening, when, on approaching Cowfield Cross, Penguin, having shaded his eyes with his hand, to obtain the better sight of the objects before him, exclaimed, " Yes, sure enough that

is Doctor Dotterel's carriage—I wonder for
what purpose it can be stopping there?—and
yonder, also, is Mr. Frampton's four-wheeled
chaise, and two or three horsemen;—that long-
necked black mare must be Frank Ringwood's
—and the parties are all confabulating together.
Very extraordinary! I must know what all
this means. Let us push forward, my young
friend; let us step briskly out, or they may
separate before we can join them." A few
minutes smart walking brought them to the
party, several of whom saluted Penguin as he
came up, and Doctor Dotterel, leaning out of
the window of his ponderous coach, drawn by
two club-tailed horses, almost as corpulent as
their owner, exclaimed, "Ha! well, I protest,
this is curious enough! Had we called a
special meeting of the neighbourhood, we
should hardly have collected more than we
have done in this accidental—hem, ha!—ren-
contre. I was mentioning, Mr. Penguin, to
my friend Ringwood, who has just joined us
—hem!—that it is incumbent upon us to put
down this approaching fair. Sir, it is, as I
may say—ahem!—an abominable nuisance!

Yes, Sir, a nuisance, promoting vice, and immorality, and profaneness, and all manner of —hem, ha!—in short, quite shocking; and as the vicar of this parish, and a magistrate, and moreover, a minister of the Gospel, I hold it to be my bounden duty—ahem!—in fact, the gentry, and all the persons of respectability— yes, Sir, of respectability—ahem! have determined to support me in suppressing it: and you, Sir, I am quite sure, will be happy to concur—that is, to assist—in short, Sir, to put it down—ahem!"

"Certainly, Doctor, certainly; all right, perfectly right," said Penguin, eagerly, not a little flattered at being thus included among the gentry and persons of respectability; "Any thing that you and the other gentlemen propose, I shall be most happy to support; and, as you very justly observe, we ought all to unite together upon an occasion of this sort."

"I see no necessity for *uniting* with any body," said the gouty and purse-proud Mr. Justinian Frampton, with a supercilious look; "but as holding one of the largest properties in this neighbourhood, and, I believe I might

say, in the whole county, exclusively of my
being a magistrate, and one of the verderers
of his Majesty's forest, I would gladly co-operate in.putting down this fair, which is little
better than an assemblage of rogues, and vagabonds, and thieves, and poachers, from whose
depredations we have already suffered quite
enough."

" 'Pon my honour, now, that's parteecularly
true," drawled Captain Frampton, the son of
the last speaker, who was driving his father
in a four-wheeled chaise. " Those dem'd poachers,—I beg pardon, Doctor Dawterel,—those
confounded poachers ruined our preserves last
season—not a phaisant to be seen ; don't know
what we shall do in October; uncawmonly dis-
agreeable—besides, a fair 's a monsous bore,
ain't it now ? Such a noise of drums and trum-
pets—and I 've enough of that, you know, when
I 'm with my raigiment. Besides, a fair 's so
vulgar, ain't it now ? abawminable ! Oh ! we 'll
put it down by all means. 'Pon my honour,
it 's quite laughable."

What was quite laughable it might have
puzzled the captain to explain, but as the word

afforded him an excuse for smiling, and displaying a remarkably fine set of teeth, he was in the habit of using it as a peroration which, whether appropriate or not, would, at least, leave his countenance, which was really handsome, in a becoming and gracious expression.

"Oh! curse the fellows!" cried one of the horsemen; "let us summon the whole *posse comitatus*, and suppress the fair by all means, if it brings any more poachers amongst us. We've been quite out of luck lately, only shot a couple of them since last February, not in these parts, at least. Some of the keepers must play booty, or they might have turned a dozen of them into dog's meat in that time. The lazy rascals won't get out of their beds if they hear a night shot."

"You will never get griping old Gideon Welbeck to consent to it," observed another horseman; "for, as lord of the manor, he gets certain fees by it; and if it only puts ten pounds in his pocket, he will uphold the fair, although, as a magistrate, it is his duty to crush it."

"We are quite aware of that," resumed the former; "but we proposed to remunerate the old curmudgeon by a general subscription, which would presently be filled."

"It is not as if there were no monied people in the neighbourhood," said the elder Mr. Frampton, with a consequential look, evidently meant to restrict that distinction to his own person.

During the latter speeches, Penguin had taken an opportunity of informing Dr. Dotterel in a whisper, that his companion, a distant connexion of his own, and the adopted son of the late Captain Tenby, of the Royal Navy, who had left him a handsome fortune, talked of purchasing an estate and settling in the vicinity of Thaxted, a communication which had such a manifest effect upon the Doctor's estimate of the stranger, that he leaned forward out of the window of his carriage, and said to Henry, with a half bow—"So I find, Mr. Melcomb, that you are likely to become one of our neighbours. Ahem! Well, I protest, it's singular that we should all meet together! And as I may look upon you as one of my future parishioners, and as a gentleman having an undoubted—ahem!—that is to say, about to hold

property in the neighbourhood; I cannot for
a moment entertain a question—in fact, a doubt,
that you will consider it your duty—yes, Sir,
your bounden duty, should you become one of
us, to co-operate in putting down this most—
ahem!—this most abominable nuisance!"

"It is not probable that I shall ever be au-
thorised to interfere in this matter," said
Henry; "but if I were, I should most certainly exercise my influence in supporting, not
in suppressing the fair, for if it be held by the
lord of the manor, as one of these gentlemen
has just observed, I doubt whether the magistrates have any legal right to interpose; and
even it be not, I am sure there could be neither
justice nor right feeling in such a measure."

"I protest, Sir, that I should be glad to
hear a reason assigned for such a very—hem!
very extraordinary opinion."

"I think the amusements of the poor, who
have most need of recreation, are already infinitely too much curtailed," continued Henry;
"and I have heard no valid reason assigned
for still farther limiting them in the present
instance. Horse races occasion a much greater

assemblage of rogues, vagabonds, and pic-
pockets, than a fair; and until I see the
gentry voluntarily suppressing the sports of the
turf, and hunting, and shooting, as well as balls,
concerts, and operas, none of which are free
from objections, I cannot lend myself to that
partial morality, which directs its indignation
exclusively against the amusements of the lower
orders. Surely the labouring classes require
relaxation more than those who never toil; and
if the magistrates must interfere at all, I should
recommend them to begin with racing, and the
sports of the field, which, as they cannot be
practised without gambling, wrangling, and
wanton cruelty, are infinitely more immoral
than the noisy merriment, or even the occasional
intemperance of a fair."

"I protest, Sir," said Dr. Dotterel, squeez-
ing himself back into his carriage with some
difficulty and a good deal of horror, "I never
in all my life heard—hem!—such unprecedented,—revolutionary,—they are, in fact, as I may
say, completely so." And turning away his
eyes from Henry, as if he considered him
unworthy of any farther notice, he continued,

addressing himself to Frank Ringwood, "You
cannot surely deny, Mr. Ringwood, the mis-
chiefs that spring from this scene of vice and
iniquity—hem!—yes, Sir, iniquity, since only
last year there was a case in *pint*"—

"In *point*," audibly ejaculated Henry.

"It so happened," pursued the Doctor, not
noticing this little interruption—"It so happened, Mr. Ringwood—how it was, I protest, I
cannot immediately discover; that is to say,
recollect,—hem!—but just at that time my carriage was mending—"

"Being mended," again interposed Henry,
as if talking to himself, and yet loud enough to
be heard by all the party.

"I cannot submit to this," said the Doctor,
reddening; "I protest it is absolutely,—nay,
worse! Good evening, Mr. Ringwood,—I will
tell you another time what I was about to state.
Mr. Frampton, I will do myself the honour of
calling at the Hall. Drive on, coachman, drive
on. Aha!—shocking! shocking!—I hope we
are not going to have any radicals in the
parish. Drive on—home! home!—hem!"

"If the gentleman held any property in the

neighbourhood,"'said Mr. Frampton, " he would
not, probably, entertain such wild and dangerous notions.   We, of the landed interest—"

" 'Pon my honour, Sir," interposed the Captain, " the dust of the Doctor's coach is quite
intawlerable,—ain't it now ?   Railly, his horses
ought not to be allowed to powder gentlemen's
trowsers in this shocking manner.   Shall I drive
on ?—Suppress racing and hunting ! Never
heard such an extror'nary proposition ; perfectly redeeculous and laughable, 'pon my honour !"
So saying, he nodded to Ringwood, displaying
his white teeth in spite of the dust, and drove
off, neither himself nor his father taking any
farther notice of Henry or Penguin.

" Gadzooks ! my young friend," cried the
latter, with a look of chagrin, " how could you
think of expressing your opinions so unguard-
edly ?   I 'm sadly afraid you have offended the
worthy Doctor, as well as Mr. Frampton ;
both of them gentlemen of the first consequence
in this neighbourhood."

" My opinion was asked ; I spoke what I
thought ; and I should have done the same had
they been emperors. In my estimation, truth

is of infinitely more consequence than either of
these gentlemen, though I am far from questioning their respectability."

"My dear Mr. Ringwood," resumed Penguin,
vexed at the evident discomposure of those who
had departed, and therefore the more anxious
to conciliate his remaining auditors, "you will,
I am sure, excuse my young friend, when I
inform you, that he is but lately arrived from
America, and has hardly had time to accustom
himself to our manners."

"Tush! neighbour, make no apologies to
me, man. I respect the young gentleman for
his honest, manly candour; and whatever I may
think of his opinions in other respects, I quite
agree with him about this foolish and tyrannical attempt at suppressing the fair, which I
shall most certainly oppose. Ay, and I should
have told the Doctor my mind very plainly, had
he not driven off in such dudgeon. Come, lads,
shall we trot? There's a heavy shower cloud-
ing up from the westward, and we shall have
wet jackets, now, before we get to Brook-
Hatch." So saying, he nodded to Penguin and
Henry, bade them good evening, and moved off

with his companions at a rapid pace; when the
geologist again took his companion to task for
his imprudence, reminding him, that whatever
latitude might be allowed in America, such
heterodox sentiments should never be unguard-
edly uttered in England, especially in the presence of the clergy and the gentry, in whom
they would be sure to cause offence; and above
all, reprehending his freedom in presuming to
correct the Doctor's English."

" If my opinions be founded in reason and
justice," said Henry, " it is precisely the clergy
and gentry who ought to hear them; because
these are the very classes whose conduct I con-
demn, in grudging every amusement to the
poor, while they cling to their own, whatever
evils they may entail; a circumstance which
subjects them to a strong suspicion of hypocri-
cy, when they assign moral motives for their
interference with all the pastimes of the lower
classes. As to the Doctor's grammatical errors,
it is surely right he should be told of them;
since he who sets up for a teacher of others,
ought not to use active participles instead of
passive."

"I tell you what, my young Domine, you will hear many blunders committed by persons in authority, in which it will much better become you to be passive than active; and, as you are a stranger among us, you will excuse my telling you, that Englishmen are instructed to respect their betters."

"In which term they are sedulously taught to include all those who are richer than themselves; an interpretation to which I can never be brought to submit. My betters in virtue and knowledge I shall always reverence as they deserve; but I cannot sacrifice my own independence to the mere claims of wealth, or even of station."

"All right, perfectly right! every man should think and act for himself; and, thank God! there is nobody more independent, more free from the control of others, than I am; but still—Gadso! it's positively going to rain. Mrs. Penguin said it would; she cautioned me not to be late; and if I should get wet twice in the same day, I shall never hear the end on't. Kind, good, careful creature! how thoughtful of her to give me the umbrella. Good night, good night! let me see you early to-morrow."

With these word Penguin started off at a long trot, which was manifestly intended to antici- pate, if possible, both the shower and the scold- ing ; while Henry, who cared not for rain, and who had no fear of angry tongues if he did not return by a given hour, quietly pursued his way back to Thaxted.

CHAPTER VI.

At last it was hinted that there could be no way so good
as that of a round robin, as the sailors call it, which
they make use of, when they enter into a conspiracy,
so as not to let it be known who puts his name first
or last to the paper.

BOSWELL's LIFE OF JOHNSON.

WHILE the gentry in the neighbourhood of
Thaxted were preparing to concert measures
for the suppression of the fair, those of the
lower orders, who anticipated either profit or
amusement from its maintenance, had not been
idle.   On the following morning, a meeting was
held in the club-room of the George-inn, for
the purpose of considering what were the most
advisable steps to be taken in vindication of
their legal rights, and for preserving the imme-

morial usages of the parish; and as it was well
known that Mr. Timothy Wicks, the landlord,
was in the habit of attending public meetings,
as well as scientific lectures, he was unanimously
voted into the chair, by a very " numerous and
respectable body " of the parishioners—such
being the character they bestowed upon their
own assemblage, in an address to the magistrates, which was subsequently agreed upon.
As the landlord had no wish whatever that the
discussion should be a dry one, he had seen
with pleasure the long table in the centre of the
room gradually covered with porter-pots, pew-
ter-gills, rummers, and glasses of all sorts; nor
had he offered any objection to the introduction
of tobacco-pipes, which, considering them as special provocatives of drinking, it was his liberal custom to bestow upon the guests for nothing. Now, however, that he was promoted
to the dignity of chairman, a sense of propriety
and decorum suggested to him that the latter
should be laid aside, as not fitting accompani-
ments for oratory; wherefore, having clamor-
ously thumped the table with a heavy pair of
lemon-squeezers till his own noise had silenced

every other, Tim, who fancied himself a little
bit of a wag as well as an orator, thus faceti-
ously opened the proceedings of the afternoon.
—" Gemmen! as I hope we are all in earnest
upon this here occasion, determined to act
upon the fulcrum, as I may, and don't mean
that our proceedings should end in smoke, I
beg to propose that we should begin by laying aside our pipes.—D 'ye catch the focus,
hey?" A loud haw! haw! attested the success
of this incipient sally, several voices exclaiming
at the same time — " Bravo, Tim! well said
Tim Wicks! that 's a good one !"—" If we sit
in such a confounded smoke and smother, we
shan't be able to hear a word that one another
says."—The chairman again plied his lemon-
squeezers, ejaculating with a voice of authority
—" Chair, chair! it 's a moral impossible we
can go on, if you won't keep order.—Tony! put
out the candle, and take away the pipes; but
gemmen will please to call for whatever they
like to drink; for we shall hear no worse, and
speak all the better, for wetting our whistles
now and then : let every man follow his own
impetus, and act upon his own equilibrio, that 's

my maximum. Gemmen! you all know what
we are met here about; and, therefore, there's
no occasion for me to fly off at the tangent of a
curve,—to speak in a parabola, which is all
the same as a problem, or parable—or to go
into all the trigonometry of a fine oration, instead of revolving upon my own circumference,
as a body may say, and sticking to my proper diameter. I wish to be solid, rather than
fluid, and never to quit—(Tony! pint purl,
gemman smock-frock. Coming Sir, coming!)—
and never to quit my proper angle of forty-five
degrees.—What are we met here for? Why,
to uphold this here fair; a question that ought
to be discussed with specific gravity, and not
lightly, as if we were only talking of a comic
section, or any thing of that sort. Gemmen!
this here's a statute fair, founded in law,
which I lay down as a vertical truth, so that
we're all rectilinear and parallel with the
horizon in supporting it, which is the ratio of
the whole radius; and whoever acts upon the
diagonal, and stirs a single cubic-foot against us,
why, he's out of the segment of the law, and
we're warranted in knocking him down with a

pendulum or a capillary tube, or any other
weapon that comes to hand.   Don't ye catch
the focus?—(Tony! quart bowl rum-punch two
gemmen never a neckcloth.   Coming, Sir, coming!)—And another thing, Gemmen;—we're
supported in this here matter by Mr. Welbeck,
who is not only the lord of the manor, but
justice of the peace and quorum, and must
surely understand the whole trigonometry of
the thing better than any body else; for in all
these cases, the impetus is proportioned to the
momentum:—that I lay down as another vertical truth, plain as a parallelogram.   Well,
Gemmen, wherever there's a maximum there's
a minimum; that's an axis that no one can
deny; and that brings me to Dr. Dotterel our
vicar, a very worthy man, no doubt, but he's
not the paradox we're all to go by; he's not to
set himself up as the polygon of the whole
place; and besides, he always joins with the
gentry—all on one side, like crooked Martha our
cook—no equilibrio about him; so far from it,
quite the reverse. D'ye catch the focus? He
may alter the Gospel, as we all know, 'cause he's
a parson; but he can't alter the law any more

than I can turn a spherical body into a round
ball, or a square into a quadrangle, both of which
are a moral impossible.—(Tony ! glass brandy-
water, Jem Penfold. Coming, Sir, coming!)—
Well, Gemmen, to come right slap-bang to the
fulcrum, there's Squire Ringwood, whose family
have been the centre of gravity to Thaxted time
out of mind—he's all for the fair, and that will
outweigh the Doctor—no, hang it ! it would
take three of him to outweigh the Doctor, speaking according to hydrostatics ; but he 's a match
for him upon the square-root, and that 's the
same thing. Then there's Mr. Frampton—
Squire Frampton as some folks call him,
he 's all agin the fair, but what of that ? He
may be as rich as a jew, but if he resorts to
violence, and goes to put down this here fair by
inert force, I maintain, as a mathematical maximum, that he understands nothing of the trigonometry of the law ; and what 's more, that he 's
no good Christian.—D'ye catch the focus, hey ?"

" Oo lie, Tim Wicks !" cried the sharp voice
of Pompey the Black from one corner of the
room. " My massa bery good Chrishun, and
he poke oo head in da fire, if oo say him not ; oo

ole talkee, talkee jackass! Dere, Tim Wicks, take dat hickory-nut for oosef to crack!"

At this flagrant insult to their chairman, and violation of all the laws of debate, a clamorous hubbub and confusion suddenly pervaded the meeting, several of the company vociferating, " Turn. him out ! turn him out !" and others making angry demonstrations for effecting that object; so that Pompey, notwithstanding his being so general a favourite, would have probably been ushered to the door or the window, with very little ceremony, had not the chairman, by stentorian shouts of " Chair ! chair ! order ! order !" seconded by the loud rapping of the lemon-squeezers upon the table, drowned the strife, and again obtained silence. All eyes were turned towards him, in expectation of what important proposition he had to offer worthy of the outrage he had received, and of such a stunning exordium, when Tim Wicks, whose eye was always first directed to his own interest, ejaculated, in a gentle voice— " Tony! a noggin-brandy, gemman in paper-cap !" a mandate so little anticipated after so pointed an insult, and so clamorous an outcry

for silence, that it was received with a loud laugh.
The prudent chairman had, in fact, been reflect-
ing, that it would be highly impolitic in the
landlord of the George-inn to offend a person
of so much wealth and influence as Mr. Frampton, or even to quarrel with his servant; wherefore, he proceeded to state, in his usual Babel
dialect, that in the observations he had felt it
his duty to make, he had intended nothing disrespectful to his worship Justinian Frampton,
Esq., one of their worthy magistrates, concluding with a hope that, after such a declaration,
Pompey would ask pardon for the offensive
expressions he had used towards himself, in
calling him an old jackass.

"Pompey ax pardon!" cried the Black:
"No, no, nebber see de day!—oo no' wish say
bad words o' my massa? den oo ten times oler
and greater jackass than ebber, to speak what
oo no mean! Dere, Tim Wicks, dere's anoder
hickory-nut for oo to crack!"

So variable is the temper of a public meeting,
that this speech, which a minute or two before
would have aggravated the general indignation,
only afforded the auditors, now that they were

once disposed to risibility, a plea for another
burst of laughter, which the chairman having
at length checked by the fresh hammering of
his lemon-squeezers, thus proceeded in his
oration.

"You may think, Gemmen, that I 've some
diagonal motive; that I don't act all together
upon the square-root, down upon the fulcrum,
as I may say, in wishing to support this here
fair; but if you do, you 're all of you turning
upon a false pivot. I stand up for our rights
and liberties; no sham segment about Tim
Wicks! I scorn to allude to my own interests,
especially as we have business enough at the
George, in a constant state of collision and percussion—in a perpetual motion—never two minutes standing upon the same centre of gravity
—toiling and moiling from morning till night;—
but, Gemmen, I feel it my duty to state, that
on the first day of the fair last year, I took ten
pounds at the tap before twelve o'clock, hard
money, Gemmen, no chalking or scoring, but
right slap-bang, point-blank, plump down upon
the fulcrum. D'ye catch the focus?"

"Ay, and by that time the stable was not

only full of horses, but the cow-house and the cart-shed too!" observed Sam Ostler, scratching his head: "that was the day our Ball threw out another spavin right inside of the near hough."

"And afore twelve o'clock o' that day, I 'd a got my breeches-pocket chuck full o' coppers, gi'n me by one gemman or another, danged if I hadn't!" said Tony the waiter, slapping his right thigh, as if to indicate the successful pocket.

"Order! order! chair!" exclaimed their master, apparently scandalized at this vain glorious boasting of his assistants.

Fat Sam Tapps, of the Cricketers, now felt it incumbent on him to state, that he, too, participated largely in the advantages of the fair; but this was by no means his motive for upholding it, being solely actuated by his regard for his neighbours, and the rights and privileges of the parish at large. The brewer's clerk stated that he was commissioned by his master to make a similar declaration; the traveller of a neighbouring distiller followed in the same strain; a pastry-cook and a victualler were

not a whit less pure and patriotic in their motives for supporting the fair—never was so disinterested, so public-spirited an assemblage. A
long and desultory conversation next ensued; as
to the measures to be adopted for maintaining
their rights; several strangers who had dropped
in, proposing resolutions, or urging proceedings of so violent a character, that the prudent
chairman thought it high time to interfere.—
" Though I am entirely of the same opinion,"
said he, " as the gemman in the brown smock-
frock at the lower end of the table, and quite
agree with the tother gemman beyond him—
him in the splashed neckcloth and greasy jacket
—as to the unlawfulness of putting down this
here fair; and think, moreover, that we ought to
show our spirit in the matter, because, according to the old proverb, ' None but the brave
deserve the fair,'—D'ye catch the focus?—
yet, howbeit, nevertheless, and notwithstanding, we must act upon the horizontal, and
not get into any legal quandary, by going
out of our own axis. For my part, I wish
to walk uprightly, and go upon the square as a
true parallelo-biped ought to do, without any

inverse ratio, or vulgar-fractions, or any thing
of that sort; and, therefore,—(Tony! gemman
calls glass of gin. Coming, Sir, coming!)—and
therefore, Gemmen, I'll read you an address to
the magistrates, drawn up by my nevy, who is
clerk to a lawyer, and therefore understands
the whole trigonometry of the matter, from the
maximum to the minimum, from the axis to
the horizon; and I think you'll all agree with
me, Gemmen, that, though it's respectively
worded, it gives the magistrates a pretty hard
hit, ay, that it does, right down, slap-bang,
point-blank, plump upon the fulcrum!"

The chairman accordingly read the address,
which, contesting the right of the magistrates to
interfere with a fair appointed by law, displayed
all the forms, technicalities, and legal expletives,
that could be stuffed into it by a pedantic lawyer's clerk, and concluded with expressing the
determination of the undersigned parishioners
to hold the fair in the usual way, paying the
customary dues to the lord of the manor, and to
repel force by force, should any attempt be
made to interfere with their lawful recreation.
As the phraseology of this paper was for the

most part utterly unintelligible, it was taken for granted that it was sound good law; the concluding resolution was at least comprehensible, and as this portion met the wish of all parties, the address was proposed and carried, *nem. con.* amidst the triumphant clattering of pewter-pots, gills, glasses, and knuckles, upon the table.— That no one might appear in the invidious light of a leader, or instigator, of these proceedings, it was agreed that the signatures should be in the form of a round robin; a measure which threatened some little graphical difficulties, until a carpenter present, placing a pewter-pot upon the paper, ran his pencil round its base, and the chairman proceeded to explain, in the clearest manner possible, that every signature should begin at the outside diameter of the circle, and describe a radii, so that the whole, when completed, should present an atmospherical shape. The majority appeared not a little bepuzzled at this darkening illustration, when an honest cartwright, after poring upon the paper, and scratching his head for a couple of minutes, exclaimed, " Heart alive, Tim Wicks! I 'll be chucked right into the horse-pond, if you don't mean that we should sign it all sloping from the round line, like the spokes of a wheel, like—"

" That 's precisely my maximum," said the chairman.

" Then why couldn't ye say so?" resumed the cartwright, " without such a mort of fine words and flummery, that are of no more use than so much shavings and sawdust. Come! shall I sign first? Bat Haselgrove ar'nt ashamed of his name."

" Write away," said the facetious chairman, a little stung, perhaps, at the reflections upon his oratory—" Write away, for as all the spokes begin at the nave, it is right that you should take the lead !"

" Haw! haw !" shouted those who under-stood the joke—" well said, Tim Wicks !" while Tony, not having comprehended the hit till the others had all done laughing, blusted out a posthumous " Haw! haw! haw! master had you there, Bat Haselgrove, danged if he hadn't !"

The process of signing, as soon as the first difficulty was overcome, proceeded fluently enough, although several, whose attention to

the more important branches of education had
prevented their acquiring the art of penman-
ship, slipped under various pretexts out of the
room; while others, disdaining flight, sturdily
observed, " it signified no odds whether they
scratched paper or not; there wasn't room for
all, their names were well known, they approved
of the address, and what they had said they
would stick to, come what would on't." There
were, in fact, enough without these parties to
complete the round robin, and though many
of the autographs evidently proceeded from men
more accustomed to hold the plough-stilts than
the pen, we can certify, from an accurate comparison of the two documents, that they were,
upon the whole, much more creditable to the
writers than the signatures of the lords spiritual and temporal to Magna Charta.

It now only remained to be settled who
should present the address to Justice Frampton,
whom it had been resolved to assail in the first
instance, since it was known that Justice Welbeck was already favourable to their cause, and
it was concluded that Dr. Dotterel, the remaining magistrate, would be entirely governed by

the decision of his wealthy friend and neighbour Mr. Framptom. Simple as it might appear, this question was not of very easy adjust-
ment, for there was too much reason to appre-
hend that the latter gentleman might take the
matter in high dudgeon, as an evidence of an
insubordinate and revolutionary spirit, and few
of the present assemblage, most of them trades-
men or persons of an inferior station, cared to
receive the first brunt of his indignation, more
especially as he was of a haughty, morose, and
arbitrary temper. Who should "bell the cat"
might not have been decided until the present
time, had not fat Sam Tapps proposed, that
they should draw lots for the performance of
the obnoxious office; a proposition which was
instantly adopted, and carried into execution,
when it appeared that the choice had fallen
upon Tony the waiter. A blank and bewildered look of alarm, a long whistling "Wheugh!"
and a simultaneous slap upon his right-thigh,
attested his first sense of this unwelcome dignity, which he seemed to relish no more than
did Falstaff " such grinning honour as Sir
Walter hath;" but ashamed of appearing

chicken-hearted before so many of his neighbours, he gathered up a long breath, and puffing it out again with a fierce look, exclaimed,
" Well, I don't care a farden, not I !—who 's
afeard ?—I 'll gi' it to un, right plump into his
own hand, danged if I don't," a resolution that
was fortified by cries of " Bravo, Tony ! Well
said, Tony !" from several of the bystanders.

At this stage of the proceedings, two additional personages entered the debating-room.
The first, who had dismounted from a beautiful blood-mare, which appeared to have travell-
ed far and fast, and which he himself had carefully installed before he entered the house,
was of rather short stature, but of remarkably
broad, muscular, almost Herculean frame, with
a face of very singular and striking appearance.
In shape it was nearly triangular, the broad
chin and jowl forming the widest part.   The
forehead was narrow, the round, black, sparkling bold eyes were set close together, the nose
was salient and well-formed, but the mouth
was disproportionately wide, while the lines, or
rather the cordage that drew his face in deep
furrows all around it, together with the dark

hue of his muzzle, well-shaven as it was, and a
profusion of black, thick curling hairs falling
down to his shoulders like a mane, imparted to
his whole 'physiognomy a pointed resemblance
to that of a lion.   Free from any fell or savage
expression, his countenance, indeed, exhibited
much of the calm, noble, imperturbable courage
observable in the look of that king of the
forest.   He wore a frock and waistcoat of dark-
coloured velveteen, blue cloth trowsers, and
enormous fisherman's boots, reaching half-way
up his thigh.   A rare India shawl was tied
round his throat, and when his waistcoat and
shirt were blown open, it might be seen that
his chest was as shaggy as that of the animal
which he so much resembled in his visage.   In
his hand he carried a rich meerschaum-pipe,
which he immediately began to smoke; nor did
any one care to tell him of the chairman's in-
terdict, all making respectful way for him as he
entered, while a buzz of " the Capt'n, the Cap-
t'n! make way for the Capt'n!" ran round the
room, and continued till he seated himself and
pursued his smoking, which he did without
uttering a word.

" Ay," observed one, " they may bring their
bum-bailies and malicious men, and what not,
to put down the fair, but if the Capt'n were to
lift up his little finger, he could soon gather a
hundred men about their ears to serve them
with sauce they wouldn't like !"

 . " Ay, and a hundred to the back of them,"
said a second.

 . " That's what he could, and a hundred to
the back of them," added a third.   There was
a momentary pause, when the Captain, taking
the pipe from his mouth, said in a loud and
deep, but calm voice,

" And a hundred more to the back of them,
—all good men, and true !" when he replaced
his pipe, and quietly resumed his puffing.

The other person who had entered the room
at the same time with the Captain, was Henry
Melcomb, who proceeded to address the assemblage, informing them that he had only just
learned the object of their meeting, or he should
have sooner attended for the purpose of giving
it his support ; condemning the illegal conduct
of the magistrates in the proposed suppression
of the fair ; recommending to his hearers to be

peaceful and orderly, but at the same time firm
in opposing it, and offering to be himself the
bearer of the address, should such be the wish
of the meeting. Henry's fearless honesty of
purpose always imparted such an earnestness to
his oratory, that it seldom failed to touch the
feelings and adapt itself to the faculties of his
auditors; while, upon the present occasion, it
offered such a contrast to the rigmarole fustian
of Tim Wicks, that his speech was received
with enthusiastic applause, and cries of "None
but the brave deserve the fair!" followed by
buzzing inquiries of, "Who is he, who is he?"
Tony, in particular, who, in spite of his assumed courage, was not a little anxious to
avoid delivering the address, not knowing to
what perils it might subject him, applauded the
speaker still more vehemently than the rest, exclaiming, "That chap's a proper good'n!—got
some pluck in him, danged if he ha'n't!" while
the Captain, taking the pipe from his mouth,
and coming towards Henry, said :—

"Lookee, Sir, I never interfere in these matters, never lift a hand nor stir a foot unless
where Government's concerned, but it does my

heart good to see any of the gentry attending a
meeting of this sort, especially a brave and
honest man, like yourself; and I, for one,
should be proud that you should carry our address, if so be you 're a parishioner or a settler
among us, for we hav'n't any of us the honour
of knowing you."

Henry confessed that he was neither the one
nor the other, an admission which, in the opinion of the meeting, rendered it impossible to
accept his offer without throwing an imputation
of cowardice upon their own body; under which
impression they recurred to their first intention
of confiding it to Tony, and Henry withdrew,
with a fresh declaration of his readiness to promote their object, whenever he could do so with
propriety.   Having been much struck with the
appearance of the Captain, as he was called, he
inquired of several who and what he was; but
could get no other answer than that it was "the
Captain," and that every body knew "the Captain" in these parts as well as they knew Thaxted Church.   Any attempt to obtain more explicit information was evaded with a look of
suspicion, and an air of mystery and reserve,

that induced him to forbear from farther inter-
rogatories, and he accordingly walked over to
Grotto-house to keep his appointment with
Penguin.

Meanwhile the proceedings at the George
suffered no interruption'; the brewer's clerk observing that it was desirable their envoy should,
for their own honour, assume as respectable an
appearance as possible, offered to lend him a
suit of clothes of his own, Tony's being by no
means of an embassadorial character ; while the
barber generously volunteered to curl his lank
hair, hitherto unacquainted with hot iron. He
retired accordingly for the purpose of com-
pleting his investiture, and upon his return into
the room, the Captain was so much amused with
his altered appearance, that he offered to treat
him with whatever he should like to drink;
observing, that he would execute his commission
all the better if he were well primed before he
went off. Tony was not slow to accept the
proffer; and at this juncture, Pompey the Black
coming forward, and declaring that he was as
staunch an advocate for the fair as any man
present, although he was Mr. Frampton's ser-

vant, promised that Tony should have immediate admission to his master the moment that
he presented himself at the Hall. This pledge
gave so much satisfaction to the Captain, that
he invited him to participate in his capacious
bowl of rum-punch before he returned home;
and as the Negro happened to have a particular
predilection for that beverage, he did not wait
to be twice solicited, but sate himself down, and
pushed in his glass, and unsheathed his white
teeth with a most radiant and cordial smile.

CHAPTER VII.

Oh! the charm that manners draw,
Nature, from thy genuine law!
Thro' benign affections, pure—
In the slight of self, secure—
If, from what her hand would do,
Or tongue utter, there ensue
Aught untoward or unfit,
Transient mischief, vague mischance,
Shunn'd by guarded elegance,
Her's is not a cheek shame-stricken,
But her blushes are joy-flushes—
And the fault, (if fault it be,)
Only ministers to quicken
Laughter-loving gaiety,
And kindle sportive wit.

WORDSWORTH.

LEAVING this party to finish their bowl, and replenish it, if they think fit, we will take the opportunity of introducing the reader to Oakham-hall, the residence of Justinian Framp-

ton, Esq. Lady Susan, the mistress of the
mansion, proud of her noble blood and ancient
family, and naturally anxious to exhibit some
excuse for her condescension in having married
a commoner, resolved that Oakham-hall, as
well as their town residence, should blazon to
all the world the great wealth of a husband,
who, if he had not been worth money, would
have been worth nothing; a fact which no one
admitted more freely than herself. Statues,
paintings, immense mirrors, costly and gorgeous
furniture, dazzling the eye by an obtrusive and
ostentatious magnificence, seemed to say on the
part of her ladyship, I married the house and
the fortune, not the man; if you wish to ap-
preciate my taste, look at the gilding and the
hangings, not at the plebeian owner of them.—
It was said of Philip the Second, when he made
a vow to build the Escurial, and dedicate it to
St. Laurence, if he won the battle of St. Quin-
tin, that the greatness of his fear might be measured by the vast extent of the structure; and
in like manner it might be affirmed of Lady
Susan, that the glittering over-finery of her
mansion attested her deep sense of the humilia-

tion she had endured in her marriage. If the splendour in which she lived furnished her an excuse, it did not afford her much consolation. Her husband was a purse-proud, consequential man, with no better redeeming point than a love of hospitality; though even this might be referred to a desire of displaying the state in which he lived, and of enjoying the good cheer in which he delighted, rather than to any inherent sociability or friendliness of disposition. Composed of such discordant elements, it may be imagined that the union had not proved a very happy one. Mutual disappointment was followed by reciprocal indifference; nor was it always that their feelings assumed even this comparative degree of comfort. Their family consisted of one son and three daughters; the former, a dissipated and coxcombical, but really elegant young man, being the Captain Frampton of whom the reader has already had a slight glimpse.

Augusta, the eldest daughter, and always the mother's favourite, because she had always promised to be a beauty, was a *blonde*, but without any of the insipidity that sometimes

accompanies that style of beauty ; her fine stature, bright blue eyes, the somewhat disdainful,
Apollo-like curl at the corners of her mouth,
and even the character of her thin, aquiline
nose, and arched nostrils, all combining to express a certain degree of hauteur, and to chal-
lenge admiration as a right, rather than to
solicit it as a favour. When to these attractions, were added a scrupulous attention to the
fluctuating elegancies of fashion in her dress,
and that indefinable air of style and distinction,
which seems to say its possessor was born to
be a duchess, to wear feathers and diamonds,
and to adorn a court, few could behold her
without an exclamation of surprise and delight
at her first appearance. After a laborious tu-
ition and drilling under a host of masters, Augusta had been sent to one of those expensive
finishing-establishments in London, where young
ladies are taught to regulate every limb and
motion, nay, every muscle and look, with an
automatic precision ; where they are instructed
by a finical, priggish, dancing-master, how to
enter and quit a room; how to curtsey in
walking, and to bow from a carriage ; how to

present or receive a card or a smelling-bottle;
how to stand, sit, or go; how to do something, nothing, and every thing, until they are
persuaded that the most insignificant action,
requires an express formula, and that every
natural movement and emotion, should be regu-
lated by artificial modifications. As nothing
is so easily seen through as these creatures of
studied management and mechanism, any observer, who once possessed a clue to Augusta's
ruling passion, which was the love of self-
display, might immediately assign the motive
of her every look, word, and action.

Unfortunately, she had not acquired these
little personal artifices from her mother, without imbibing also much of her cold, haughty,
and ambitious character. Remembering the
constant mortifications she had herself endured
from having married a commoner, and confiding in the power of her daughter's charms,
Lady Susan had determined that she should
be at least a countess; and Augusta, equally
proud of her mother's noble relations, and of
her father's wealth, willingly lent herself to
the belief that she might command a titled

husband, under which conviction, she looked down upon all suitors of inferior rank with an ill-concealed disdain. Several of this class had, indeed, been refused, and no more commoners presented themselves; while the lords and lordlings hung most provokingly back. This might not have happened, had Lady Susan possessed art enough to conceal her art; but she angled so palpably for a title, that the young noblemen either shunned the bait altogether, or only played around it to laugh at it, and defy its allurements. Her Ladyship, and her ambitious projects, became a sort of by-word among them; that most anti-connubial of all feelings, a sort of compassionate ridicule, was excited by the daughter's manifest participation in her plans; a young collegian dubbed her with the unfortunate nickname of the Tuft-hunter; and at the period of our history, Miss Frampton had lost the first bloom of her youth and novelty, had satiated the town with the display of her beauty, and was infinitely less likely to obtain the great object of her life, than she had been at the dazzling outset of her career.

Fanny, who was several years younger than Augusta, had in early life laboured under some apparent disadvantages, which ultimately proved to be her greatest blessings. Inferior to her sister in personal beauty, she had been an object of comparative indifference to her mother, and had thus escaped the baneful influence of all her stratagems, sophistications, and ambitious manœuvres, until she was old enough to detect and reject them; while her delicate state of health not allowing her to be put in regular training at a polite seminary, her natural character had been permitted to develope itself in the progress of such education as she received at home. Illness had necessitated occasional interruptions of her studies, and her mother's neglect had left her at intervals to prosecute or abandon them, just as she thought fit; but an innate genius and singular quickness of apprehension enabled her to acquire, by a sort of intuition, that which others can only obtain by long and laborious application; while her lucky escape from the perpetual artifice and discipline to which her sister had been subjected, had left her, what she was intended to be by Nature, an

unaffected, simple, warm-hearted, sportive girl.
She neither paused to calculate how she should
look, nor what she should say; and yet, with all
this nonchalance and submission to the impulse
of the moment, she never committed an inde-
corum, never threw herself into an ungraceful
attitude, never uttered an unbecoming sentiment. She was darker than her sister, and
without being so regularly handsome, was infinitely more lovely and fascinating. Augusta's
stately beauty could neither bend nor alter.
Fanny's was playful and fluctuating. One was
like the trained and grafted French rose, tall
and majestic, but with a stiff, formal, artificial aspect in the midst of its beauty; the
other resembled the same flower, with all its free
and natural graces, hanging in careless elegance,
and swinging as the wind directs it. Fanny's
countenance had acquired no tricks, it never
wore an assumed expression, and rarely concealed an emotion that she felt. All this open
singleness of heart was so contrary to the conventional forms, the guarded concealments, and cold
etiquette of high life, that it gave prodigious
offence to Lady Susan; who having in vain en-

deavoured to correct it, at length abandoned the attempt, observing, that she should never be able to make any thing of poor Fanny; that she was a mere giddy, giggling girl, and would always remain so. Fanny was content to wear the character they had assigned to her, provided she might escape from a constant disguise and constraint which she found insupportably irksome, and indulge occasionally in a little malicious pleasantry at her sister's expense: but this giddy girl would sometime hazard a remark, or elicit a trait of feeling, that showed her to be any thing but what they termed her.

On the morning, when we have introduced our readers to Oakham-hall, Dr. Dotterel and his sister had called to pay a visit. The latter, an old maid, somewhat stricken in years, and, like her brother, inclined to corpulency, lived at the vicarage, where she superintended the household arrangements, and piqued herself upon discharging in her own person all those duties of a good old English hospitable housewife, which the fine ladies of the present day are so apt to delegate to housekeepers and servants. Although a little starch and prudish, she was a good-tem-

pered woman, of feeble understanding, and consequently of narrow notions, with a particular abhorrence of innovation of any sort, and
more especially of the march of intellect, her
own having remained tolerably stationary from
her earliest years. In these particulars, as
well as in her personal appearance, she bore a
strong resemblance to her brother; so much so,
as to have called forth the sarcastic observation
from Lady Susan, that if both wore petticoats,
it would be impossible to distinguish one old
woman from the other. The Doctor, however,
had several excellent points about him; it was
his head not his heart that was narrow, and the
kindness of the latter generally proved too
strong for the old-fashioned notions of the for-
ner, so that if he seldom said a liberal thing, he
never did an illiberal one: a better inconsistency, since actions are of much more consequence to the community than opinions, than if
he had reversed the proposition. Measures or
individuals that he the most condemned, were
the most sure of his assistance, if they appealed
to his charity or his kindly feelings of any sort;
and it was sometimes amusing to hear him in-

vent excuses for the amiability that occasioned
his good deeds to be so frequently opposed to
his less generous declarations. Mr. Frampton's
whole family was collected in the great drawing-room at the time these visitants called. He
himself reclining in an arm-chair, with his gouty
foot upon an embroidered velvet cushion, retained his position, patiently awaiting whatever might happen. " Those horrid Dot-
terels!" exclaimed Lady Susan, as soon as she
heard their names announced : " what can they
be coming for again? surely they called here
last"—and then stepping forward with a smile
of the most cheerful welcome, she continued,
" My dear Miss Dotterel, my good Doctor,
this is really kind of you, I am quite delighted
to see you!—and both looking so well—pray be
seated."

Miss Frampton being slightly indisposed
with a cold, and not wearing in consequence
her best looks, placed herself with her back to
the light, assumed her reception smile, made
the prescribed half bow and half curtsey, drew
herself slowly up again, and reseated herself in
such a way as to display a portion of her well-

turned leg and ankle, carefully set off by an
open-work French silk-stocking, and a Parisian
shoe of the last importation.

"Delighted to see you, 'pon my honour!" said
the Captain, lightly throwing up his curls with
one hand, while he surveyed his whole figure
in an opposite mirror with a complacent earnestness that showed he experienced much more
delight in seeing himself than his visitants.

Fanny, who really liked both the Doctor and
his sister for their goodness of heart, in spite of
their little oddities and old-fashioned notions,
ran towards them as they entered, warmly
pressed their hands, and welcomed them with
a cordial smile infinitely more expressive than
words. No sooner was Miss Dotterel seated,
than not being provided with any immediate observation, and deeming movement of any kind
a sort of relief from entire silence, she began
to fidget about in her chair, and adjust her
clothes, so as to make the rustling of her an-
tique silk gown, as was her wont, a momentary
substitute for conversation. While thus occupied, and clearing her throat at the same time
that it might be ready for action, her eye fell

upon Miss Frampton's leg, which being exposed, as she thought, rather more than strict
decorum warranted, she pulled down her own
petticoats over her thick, cotton-clad ankles
with an alarmed and squeamish look, intending
it as a friendly hint to her neighbour. Augusta
understood the implied meaning of the action,
but without altering her position, continued
talking with her brother, who whispered in his
usual drawling way—" Shocking pity, ain't it
now, to hide those taper legs of Miss Dotterel's ? capital models for a couple of mill-
posts ! never saw any thing like them except her
sister, the doctor's, a palpable plagiarism—quite
redeculous, 'pon my honour."

Lady Susan was at the moment catechising
Fanny, *sotto voce*, about some article of dress
which had not been arranged *selon les regles;*
Mr. Frampton had engaged the Doctor in conversation, and Miss Dotterel at length deeming
it indispensable that she should signify her presence, and determined to commence with an interesting theme, exclaimed, " Brother, you were
asking me about the apricots on the stand-
ard tree down by the pigeon-house. Well, I

counted sixty-two yesterday, and would you
believe it, there were only forty this morning!
The others must have been all blown down by
the wind in the night, but I could only find
sixteen, and those I put in one of the willow-
pattern dishes, and sent Davy with them to
Mrs. Penguin; for several of them were bruised,
and none of them would keep, and she has
been very civil to us lately in sending us that
nice preserved-ginger that you are so fond of,
otherwise I know you don't like to part with
any of our fruit. Lady Susan, have you made
your preserves and your raspberry vinegar yet?
It *is* a troublesome job, now isn't it? and I'm
sure I'm glad ours is all over."

"I am truly sorry I cannot inform you,
having quite forgotten to ask Mrs. Jellicolt
about it," replied Lady Susan, with a courteous
smile, while, as she caught Augusta's eye, she
threw up her own with an expression of contemptuous derision.

"La! how very odd!" exclaimed Miss
Dotterel.

"Most extr'or'nary!" said the Captain;
"couldn't railly have supposed her Ladyship

to be ignorant of such an important fact; could you, Fanny?"

Sportive as she was, and ever ready to join any raillery or bantering among themselves, Fanny could not be drawn in to assist in quizzing their present visitors, and she therefore stated, with a very serious face, that she had heard Mrs. Jellicolt express her intention of beginning the preserves on the following day. Miss Dotterel had commenced a very minute description of her own particular method of potting apricots, when the Doctor, having finished a long discussion with Mr. Frampton respecting a game of whist at their last meeting, interrupted her by exclaiming—

"Dorothy, our friends don't want to hear any such trifling matters; we can talk about the apricots another time;" a hint which immediately silenced the affectionate and submissive sister, who was not unaccustomed to such checks, and always deferred to them. "I came over on purpose to mention to you, Mr. Frampton," continued the Doctor, " only the game of whist put it out of my head, that I had a very early visit this morning from our neighbour,

Mr. Penguin,—ahem!—to make explanations touching the conduct of this young man, Mr. Melcomb, whose opinions last night, when we encountered him on the road, did appear to me completely—ahem!—and I have no doubt they struck you in the same light; did they not?"

Not always having his words at command, although he spoke slowly and pompously enough, the Doctor, whenever he boggled for an expression, would substitute a pause or a "hem!" for the required term, proceed in his discourse as if he had uttered it, and take it for granted that his auditors understood him as well as if he had. Aware of this habit, and not wishing to send back so slow a finder in search of the missing word, Mr. Frampton declared that the sentiments alluded to had made precisely the same impression upon himself; when the Doctor proceeded; "Mr. Penguin, explained to me, that the young man had not the most remote idea, that is to say, not the smallest thought of giving offence,—ahem!—but that being, as I may say, though not born in that country, an American—"

"A Yankee, is he?" interposed Mr. Frampton; "that's not in his favour—I don't like any of them—they are little better than revolutionists and rebels!"

"Very true," observed Miss Dotterel; "and I fear they have not a jot of religion among them. How can they, indeed, without an established church and tithes?"

"Impossible, quite impossible! shocking! shocking!" ejaculated the Doctor, shaking his head with a look of reprobation; "but I once knew an American, nevertheless, who played an excellent rubber."

"And it must be confessed," added the sister, anxious to do justice even to a people without tithes, "that their cranberries are finer than ours. When I was last at Southampton, I bought a small cask at Jefferson and Hacklestone's, the sign of the Golden Canister, and of all the cranberries I *ever*—"

"Dorothy! Dorothy! we can talk of them at the same time as the apricots," said the Doctor.—"Certainly, Mr. Frampton, it is bad, very bad; in short, a complete—ahem!—as I freely confess, that this young gentleman should have been educated in America, but as he may

get over, in short, get rid of all these heretical
—yes, Sir, heretical notions; as he is about to
settle in this neighbourhood, and is, moreover,
as I am given to understand, a person of large
fortune, I have consented to overlook, in short,
to take no farther notice, as I may say, of our
little—ahem!—yesterday, and, in fact, to be
introduced to him."

" Nay, Doctor, that alters the affair altogether," said Frampton, who, for his own sake,
never chose to undervalue the importance of
wealth : " if he is a person of large fortune, he
must, of course, be perfectly respectable, and
a desirable acquaintance; and as I presume
others will be entirely governed by me, I shall
be happy to give him a passport into the first
society of this part of Hampshire, by receiving
him at Oakham-hall."

" I must request, Mr. Frampton," said Lady
Susan, " that you will decide on nothing of this
sort hastily, or without my concurrence. At
your solicitation I consented to receive those vulgar Penguins, and I have repented it ever since."

" Surely, Lady Susan, you must yourself

admit that his East India Madeira is in comparable, his dinners are excellent, and as to his Staffordshire puddings—"

"I wish he would stay at home and eat them," interposed her Ladyship, " and not wander about the country in that ridiculous geological-dress, as he calls it. He had the presumption to approach the carriage t'other day, as I was riding with my cousin, Sir Nugent Clavering, and was about to address me, when I threw sixpence out of the window, as if I had mistaken him for a beggar, and desired the coachman to drive on."

"La! how very odd!" exclaimed Miss Dotterel. "Well, I found sixpence myself last Tuesday fortnight. It was the time we were brewing our table-ale: I had gone out at the orchard-gate, and was crossing the road to call at Laurence Penfold's to order some more hops, when who should come by but Sam Holden, driving along in his taxed-cart, drawn by that vicious black horse of his — you know his horse I dare say, Lady Susan; so I drew up on one side—"

"Dorothy! Dorothy! put the sixpence in the same basket with the apricots and cranberries," cried the Doctor.

The good gossip again looked at her brother with an affectionate smile, and held her peace.

"And Mrs. Penguin is a thousand times worse than her husband," said Miss Frampton. "If she were only vulgar she might be endured; but she is low, which is intolerable. It is really overwhelming in hot weather to see her flaring hat and red feathers, her red thick fingers loaded with rings, and her fine clothes put on 'over that, and over that, and over that,' like Betty Blackberry's, as if it were the depth of winter."

"We could not, of course, notice such people in London," said Mr. Frampton; "but as a magistrate, and the principal person in this neighbourhood, if I did not receive them at Oakham-hall, nobody would visit them; which was my sole consideration in wishing Lady Susan to leave cards at Grotto-house, and to keep up a certain degree of acquaintance."

"To say nothing of the East India Madeira, and the Staffordshire puddings," whispered

Augusta to her brother, neither of them ever scrupling to ridicule their father.

"Very good, very good; not the puddings, but the observation. You're in high force, Augusta, this morning;—quite redeeculous, 'pon my honour!" returned the Captain, presenting his enamelled snuff-box to his nose, so as to display his white hand and glittering rings, and then returning it to his pocket.

"For my part," observed Fanny, "I think we ought to be grateful to the Penguins for favouring us with an occasional visit, since it never fails to relieve the dullness of Oakham-hall with a little amusement, and to afford us at least a laugh, which we rarely hear, unless when some of Pompey's tricks occasion one to echo up the staircase from the servants' hall."

"I'm sure, child, you laugh often enough yourself, though I have frequently repeated to you Lord Chesterfield's opinion of that vulgar emotion. Indeed, you sometimes appear to indulge in it out of opposition, and absolutely to laugh at nothing."

"No, indeed, I am rarely without an excuse; for I cannot help laughing at our own solemn

and stately gravity; and it is precisely because
Mr. Penguin breaks in upon all this, and seems
to have no respect for it, that I like him."

"How comes it that you always like the vul-
garest people best?" inquired Augusta.

"I suppose, sister, because they are the most
natural and amusing. I know so completely
by heart all our polite and titled visitants, who
call, speak, and look by routine, that I could
tell you beforehand every word they would
utter, and every expression they would wear,
with as much certainty as I can tell what o'clock
it is by casting my eye upon the dial-plate."

"I protest, Miss Fanny," said Dr. Dotterel,
"I hope you don't include me in this polite list,
for I flatter myself I am not to be so easily read,
—a little more variety in my discourse, I hope,
and in fact I trust. To do this, you must not
only possess great discrimination, but be, as I
may say, a complete—ahem!—don't you think
so, Miss Augusta?"

"You have exactly expressed my own sentiments," replied Miss Frampton, bowing to the
Doctor, and casting a side glance at her brother.

"And mine too," said the Captain. "Most

extr'or'nary coincidence ; the very phrase that
was on the tip of my own tongue, 'pon my
honour! But you 're wrong, Fanny, to re-
deecule any of our visitants, whether genteel or
vulgar ; it 's a thing I never do myself—quite
abawminable ; don't you think it is, Miss
Dotterel ?"

"Why, to tell you the truth, I was a *leetle*
surprised at Miss Fanny's observation. To be
sure, present company 's always excepted, you
know ; but I must say for myself, that no one
can tell beforehand what I am going to talk
about, can they, brother? Just at this time o'
year, indeed, one naturally talks of what 's going
on in the great world—of jams, and jellies, and
preserves, and such like ; and that reminds me
of a question I had intended to ask you, Lady
Susan, whether you have made your ketchup
yet, for we can't get any good mushrooms at
the Vicarage."

"And that reminds me," said Lady Susan,
evading the question, by turning the subject,
"that we have wandered from the point at
which we started, as to this Mr. Henry Melcomb, whom it is wished to introduce at the

Hall. Who is he? whence is he? what is he?"

" The two former questions become of very little consequence, when we can answer the latter, by stating that he is rich," said Mr. Frampton.

" You can hardly expect *me* to forget the value and importance of birth and rank, whatever may be your own opinion," said Lady Susan, haughtily; " though I am quite willing to allow the secondary importance of wealth. Who has seen this Mr. Melcomb? What is he like?"

" A remarkably handsome young man, I protest," said the Doctor; " though I cannot say I was pleased with his notions altogether, nor indeed with his—ahem!"

" As to those," remarked the Captain, " I never attended to them; though I remember he talked some nonsense: quite redeeculous; now railly wasn't it? about putting down horse-races and the opera; but I couldn't keep my eyes from his dress, 'pon my honour! I don't know what sorts of coats gentlemen may wear in America, but I wouldn't exhibit such an article myself in any of the streets of Lon'on, for a farthing less than a thousand pounds. A most Trans-atlantic turn-out—irresistibly ludicrous—can't help laughing when I think of it."

Mr. Frampton and the Doctor becoming now deeply engaged upon the important subject of the fair, Miss Dotterel, moving her chair close to Lady Susan, and carefully covering her ankles, an action which generally accompanied every change of position, resumed her inquiry about the ketchup; and then, in a most confidential whisper, proceeded to give her Ladyship an account of the funeral of old Isaac, a poor villager who had recently been buried, of the little property he had left behind him, and of the silver-watch he had bequeathed to Sally Wicks.

After two or three ineffectual attempts to escape from this infliction, Lady Susan, fixing her eyes on the splendid clock upon the mantel-piece, exclaimed with an assumed look of surprise, " Almost three o'clock, I declare !"

" La! so it is," said her tormentor, not in the least taking the hint; " but I 've nothing particular to do this morning, for I 've finished my preserves and ketchup, thank Heaven ! and we don't dine till five. You 've got a new French clock, haven't you? What a beauty! I never saw any thing so handsome!"

" It *ought* to be handsome, madam!" cried Mr. Frampton, whose ear quickly caught any admiration of his gorgeous finery, and who measured every thing by what it had cost. "There is nothing, I flatter myself, at Oakhamhall, that is not of the very best and most expensive kind."

The Doctor, notwithstanding frequent syncopes of speech, had contrived to make his auditor understand that it was absolutely necessary to suppress this formidable fair, and to compel the lower orders to submit to the wills of their pastors and masters, who were so much richer, and, consequently, so much more respectable than themselves; sentiments in which Mr. Frampton so perfectly coincided, that he puffed out his cheeks with mingled complacency at his own importance, and indignation against those who would presume to oppose it; when the door suddenly opened, and, without the announcement of any new visitant, a strange figure bolted into the centre of the apartment. It was Tony, the bearer of the address voted at the George, but not less disguised by his borrowed habiliments and the efforts of the barber, than by the potent contents of the frequently replenished bowl, in which he had been allowed to participate. Sobered to a certain extent by finding himself, for the first time in his life, in so grand a room, and among so many of the gentry, he remained for some seconds bowing very reverentially. His form was reflected by the numerous long mirrors surrounding him ; and being utterly unable to recognise his proper figure in its present transmogrified state, he thought that he beheld so many of the inmates greeting and welcoming him to Oakham-hall; under which impression he kept making profound bows to himself, turning round and round, like a dog pursuing his own tail, and exclaiming at the same time, " Sarvant, Sir, sarvant; this is kind on ye to receive a body so hearty like, dang'd if it baint!" While thus backing and bowing, he bumped against a marble statue of Minerva, standing on a low pedestal, and starting round, ejaculated, " Ax your pardon, ma'am ! Lord! Lord! ye be as white in the feace as our Ball!—I hope

I haven't frought ye: take my arm, ma'am, if you want to step down." And he held up his hand, thinking, probably, that the lady had jumped upon the pedestal to get out of his way.

Miss Frampton, who was seated close beside it, had, however, no sooner caught his eye, than he quitted the statue, placed himself opposite to her, and surveying her with the maudlin and fond look of intoxication, continued, " Adad! you're a jolly wench, handsomer nor Molly Stubbs, danged if ye baint!"

" Good heavens! who is this strange creature, and what does he mean?" cried Augusta, in some alarm.

" Lord love ye!" continued Tony, " don't ye be frought; I'm a friend to the fair."

" Fellow! fellow!" cried Mr. Frampton, sternly, " it appears to me that you have been making a beast of yourself."

" Thank ye, Sir, kindly; and I hope you're the same," replied Tony, again bowing with great respect.

" Speak, booby!" exclaimed the Doctor, " What do you want?—are you drunk?"

" No, parson; are you?" responded the

clown, with a look and tone of honest inquiry, as if he really considered it a matter of doubt.

Hitherto the rest of the company had stared at these inexplicable proceedings, as if they had been transfixed with amazement; but Lady Susan, beginning now to comprehend that the intruder was intoxicated, called angrily to her son, bidding him throw the horrid fellow out of window, or kick him down stairs.

" Railly, now," replied the Captain, " I am the last person to be fasteedious upon an occasion of this natur; but pawsitively the creature smells so abawminably of rum, a leequor to which I have a most parteecular objection, that I must decline being personally concerned in his ejectment; must indeed, 'pon my honour! We have plenty of people, however, who will see him speedily conveyed to the horse-pond." And he rang the bell to summon some of the servants for that purpose.

Tony, in the meanwhile, finding the address in his hand, and being determined to present it to some one, advanced towards Mr. Frampton, mumbling, as he tendered it to him, " Sarvant, your worship, sarvant, Sir. I do ax leave to

hand you, right into your own paw, as I said I
would, this here address, whereby you'll see
that we mean to keep up the fair; and having
the law on our side, I'm desired to say, with
the respects and submission of the whole parish,
that we don't care a farden for your worship,
nor for Doctor Dotterel neither."

"Sirrah! sirrah!" cried Mr. Frampton, reddening and swelling with anger, "you shall be
set in the stocks for this insolence to a magistrate, and a person of my consequence."

"No, but I sha'n't though: got the law o'
my side, danged if I haint! so I don't care a
brass button for your worship," cried Tony;
who having now completely recovered his confidence, set his arms a-kimbo, and looked most
stolidly resolute.

"I protest," exclaimed Dr. Dotterel, "this
is most audacious behaviour; in fact it is, as I
may say, a complete case of—ahem! This fellow ought to be horse-whipped; such conduct
really beats every thing."

"Ah, like enough, but nobody sha'n't beat
me. You baint in the pulpit now, Muster
Parson; and so, having the law on my side, I

shouldn't mind fighting ye for a gallon of beer, danged if I should! Hurra! None but the brave deserve the fair!"

In this interval the bell had been rung several · times with increased vehemence, and, as Tony was evidently becoming pot-valiant and pugnacious, all eyes were turned towards the door with considerable anxiety, when it at length flew open, and Pompey the Black, still more decidedly under the influence of the rum-punch than his friend Tony, reeled into the room, singing or rather shrieking,

" 'Tis Saturday night, wid a hi! hi!
   'Tis Saturday night, wid a ho!
   Da market he done, and da nigger he run,
   To dance round and round to da Banjore's sound;
   Den all clap hands, and jump and sing,
   Hi! ho! tink a ting-ting!"

Clapping his hands and jumping, as he shouted the last lines, he looked round him with a smile, which drew up the thick curtain of his lips from his white teeth, and betrayed at the same time, by its vacant expression, that he was utterly unconscious what he was about.

"How, sirrah!" exclaimed his master, "what's

the meaning of this ?　Do you forget where you
are ? . Take this drunken fellow, who has found
his way into the drawing-room, and kick him
instantly down-stairs."

"Gorry-mirree !" exclaimed Pompey, " who
ebber tink o' dat ?　Tony, ma friend, him dam
good fellow, him lub rum-punch, and nebber
drink warra; but him no more drunk dan mysef,
debble a bit !　Pompey and Tony, um dance
to-gedder, all the same, like two grasshopper.
Hi ! ho ! tink a ting-ting !"　In the awkward
capers that accompanied these words, he kicked
away the stool on which was propped the gouty
foot of his master, who, snatching up his leg
with a shout of pain, and, at the same time,
seizing his crutch-headed stick, prepared to
launch it at the head of the offender.　But
morose as he naturally was, and irritated by his
present sufferings, he could never forget that the
black had once saved his life at the risk of his
own, so that he quietly replaced the stick, rubbed
his foot, and contented himself with exclaiming,
"Confound the rascal ! — the poor fellow, I
mean ; he doesn't know what he is about, or

he would rather break his own limbs than hurt mine."

"Mr. Frampton! Mr. Frampton!" cried Lady Susan, who hated the Negro, "I always told you he would one day be the death of you, if you kept this odious black wretch in the house."

"What, da debble!" cried Pompey, indignant at such an imputation, even in the midst of his drunkenness; "Me be de dess of ma massa! and I da same Pompey what fotch um up fom da bottom of da sea, when um got no more speesh in um's mous dan a droun rat! Black wresh! oo black wresh ooself to tink me sush bad mans; so dere's a hickery-nut for oo to crack!" His complacency, however, quickly returned, for suddenly advancing towards Miss Dotterel, he chucked her familiarly under the chin, to her inexpressible consternation, and then seizing her hand, exclaimed, with a most fond, fuddled, and asinine look, "What oo say, missee? oo danse da Jumbee-Jumbee dance wid Pompey? Oo rader ole, and little bit ugly, and bery hebby and lumpy; but neber mind, jump op and stir

you stum, ole one, and once oo begin, oo danse
all da same like da fat big porpus when um
flounder in da warra. Hi! ho! tink a ting-
ting!"

"Hurra! none but the brave deserve the
fair!" echoed Tony, balancing on his totter-
ing knees, and holding out his hands to the
Black for a renewal of their wild dance, to the
infinite dismay of the company. The horrified
Miss Dotterel had already waddled out of the
room, ejaculating, "O the filthy animal!—to
be chucked under the chin for the first time in
my life, and the creature to be a black!" The
other females were preparing to follow her example, when the Captain, who had gone in
search of the men-servants, and had found them
all assembled in the court-yard, gaping at the
performances of Punchinello, arrived to the
rescue with a timely reinforcement. The butler
took charge of Tony, who quietly suffered himself to be led out of the room, shouting at the
same time, "None but the brave deserve the
fair!" while Joseph, a stout under-servant,
firmly collared Pompey, who showed a disposition to resist this summary process, until he

should have completed the Jumbee-Jumbee
dance. Joseph, however, hauled him away, the
black wriggling and giggling, and expostulating
with him as he retired, "Hosepp! Hosepp! oo
comical dog! what oo bout? Gog! how oo
tickle ma troat wid oo dam knuckles! Hosepp,
I say!"—Doctor Dotterel called lustily after
the servants to secure both offenders, that they
might be set in the stocks for drunkenness; but
Mr. Frampton limited his threats to Tony,
saying, that he would himself take care to
punish Pompey. In England, however, a
drunken man is sure to excite a good-humoured
smile, and awaken the sympathy of the lower
order, a feeling of which the present delinquents found the advantage, for the servants,
who were moreover all staunch advocates for
the fair, dismissed Tony scot free, to find his
way back to the George, and inducted Pompey
to his own room, that he might sleep himself
sober.

CHAPTER VIII.

> There was a love-born sadness in his breast,
> That wanted stimulus to bring on rest ;
> These simple pleasures were no more of use,
> And danger only could repose produce ;
> He join'd th' associates in their lawless trade,
> And was at length of their profession made.
>
> CRABBE.

NOTWITHSTANDING the ill-timed intoxication of Tony and of the Black ally by whom he had been admitted into Oakham-hall, the Captain, who had treated them at the George, was too veteran a practitioner upon bowls of punch, to be in the smallest degree affected by his own potations, or even to suspect that his companions could be injured by what appeared to him to be very temperate draughts. After their departure, therefore, be mounted his black blood mare, and still retaining his meerschaum-

pipe in his mouth, shortened by taking out
some of the joints that composed it, struck at
a brisk pace across the country towards the
New Forest, into the wild recesses of which he
quickly plunged. The real name of this man
was Lawrence Boulderson, though he had long
ceased to be saluted by either of those appellations. Born in the Forest, his father, one of
the under-keepers, who had charge of an extensive walk, employed him for some years
in brouzing and feeding the deer, cutting and
faggoting underwood, or watching for deer-
stealers and other trespassers upon his walk;
but the youth had an innate predilection for
the sea; the sight of the numerous vessels coast-
ing the Isle of Wight channel, or passing round
the Needles, which he could distinctly see from
the high ground of his ordinary station, corroborated this tendency, and an accidental connexion with a band of smugglers, who had a
concealed store in the haunts of the New Forest,
enabled him to gratify it. His natural affections, however, which were strong, retained him
for some time at home, until his father, a stern
violent man, having unmercifully punished him

for some trivial offence, his proud bold heart
revolted from the injustice, he quitted the pa-
ternal roof, and joining the smugglers, was not
only allowed to indulge the long-cherished
wishes of his bosom by being sent to sea, but
was gradually initiated in all the mysteries, and
inured to all the hardships and dangers of the
lawless career upon which he had entered. For
this mode of life, one that requires a rare union
of almost incompatible qualities, in order to
prosecute it with a fair chance of safety and
success, he seemed to be so especially qualified
by nature, as almost to justify the hyperbolical
praise of one of his friends, who declared that
he must have been born a smuggler; considering that character not in its paltry details, to
which any sorry rogue may be competent, but
with reference to its more enlarged, complex,
and mercantile operations. Capable of every
endurance, whether of fatigue or privation,
absolutely insensible to fear, and yet discreet
and cautious in encountering danger; never
known to be intoxicated—a circumstance, however, which might rather be attributed to the
singular strength of his constitution, than to

his temperance; as acute and judicious in planning an exploit, as he was undaunted and indefatigable in executing it; and above all, so unimpeachable in his integrity, that he would rather deny himself his own fair share, than defraud an employer or a colleague, it may easily be supposed that the superiority of his mind quickly manifested itself, and that he rapidly rose through all the gradations of employment, until he finally became the leader of that band which he had joined as a boyish volunteer.

As his means and his confidence increased, his operations, though always confined to the illicit or *free* trade, as its followers term it, assumed something of a mercantile character. He was connected, indeed, with several eminent merchants in London, for whom he had executed delicate and difficult commissions during the war, either by the conveyance of important information from one coast to the other, or by the transport of guineas and other valuable freightage to and fro; in all which tempting situations he had never violated the confidence reposed in him, never done any thing calculated

to impugn the general opinion of his united
boldness and address.   Such was the line of
life in which he had now been engaged for
many years and with varied success, sometimes
as an agent for others, though more often, latterly, upon his own exclusive account; but as
such an illegal career could hardly be pursued
with impunity, all his wariness and ingenuity
had not enabled him to elude the vigilance of
the law. He had been repeatedly arrested,
tried, and condemned to various fines and im-
prisonments, while warrants and capiases for
the various penalties he had incurred, sometimes
outstanding against him to the amount of many
thousand pounds, had compelled him more
than once to fly the country.   Not less generous and humane than intrepid, he made it a
rule to abstain from blood and violence, except
when they were forced upon him in self-defence,
often exposing and surrendering his own person
to screen his comrades, or to protect his an-
tagonists when they were overpowered; so that
if he was engaged in any desperate affray, his
individual conduct seldom failed to command
the esteem even of those who were opposed to

him: For the purpose of perplexing or baffling the law, in case of being subjected to prosecution, it is customary with all smugglers to drop their real names and assume an alias, or a nickname, frequently one of a ludicrous description, consonant to the appearance or supposed character of the wearer. Boulderson had for many years alternately borne the appellations of Blacklocks, from his profusion of dark curling hair, and of Lion, from his strong resemblance to that noble animal; but latterly, since he had become by tacit consent of the whole fraternity along the coast, a sort of general leader and manager in all important enterprises, he had received the distinctive, honorary title of " The Captain," by which he was familiarly addressed, in all the ports from the Land's End to Yarmouth; even the King's officers, to most of whom he was known, and by whom, notwithstanding his avowed profession, he was generally respected, invariably bestowing that appellation upon him. Without any dereliction of their duty, many of the latter were upon the most amicable terms with him. Theirs was a mutual contest of courage and

cunning, but one which, like any other generous
warfare, was not incompatible with a certain
degree of friendliness among the individuals
waging it.   This was the light in which the
Captain loved to view it, for he always considered himself as a sort of legitimate belli-
gerent, pitted avowedly against the King's
revenue officers, but in all other respects as
loyal, honest, and orderly a subject, as any in
the realm.   Upon the continent, where the
untoward state of his affairs had occasionally
compelled him to be a resident, he was as much
at home, even in the midst of the war, as if he
had been in England; and the " English Lion,"
for such was his continental *sobriquet*, had
smoked his pipe with Mynheers, Burgomasters,
and Frenchmen, and was as perfectly well
known upon almost every exchange from the
Texel to Cherburg, as he was along all the
southern shores of his native island.

Exclusively of his numerous confederates
along shore, and his acquaintance with all the
fishermen, most of whom were ready to assist,
now and then, in "running a crop of goods,"
or doing "an odd job in the free trade;" he

was in immediate fellowship and league with
a band of landsmen, as resolute and sturdy
abettors of his enterprises, as any of the regular smugglers. These were the tenants of
that multitude of cabins and cottages, run up
in defiance of trespass, upon the borders and
purlieus of the New Forest; a set of men, who,
in addition to the advantages of rearing cattle
and hogs upon its commons and waste lands,
found occasional employment in cutting furze,
and conveying. it to the brick-kilns, but who,
having no regular returns of weekly labour to
subsist on, were generally poor and profligate,
and depended, for their collateral support, upon
deer-stealing, poaching, purloining timber, and
assisting, whenever their services were required,
in running spirits or other goods ashore, after
they had been floated up Southampton-water,
or the forest rivers, for the purpose of conceal-
ment within its coverts and recesses. Most
of these dispersed bands could be assembled
at a given point, and at a short notice, whenever any important enterprise required a con-
centration of their forces. The captain had
numerous emissaries, while he himself, riding

a thorough-bred mare which defied pursuit,
and possessing a fast-sailing cutter, which could
outstrip any vessel in the King's service, had
the means of issuing his orders with a celerity
and secrecy that generally baffled discovery,
although his plans were occasionally defeated
by accident or treachery. It was not, therefore, a vain-glorious boast, when he had asserted at the George-inn, that by holding up his
little finger, he could collect some hundreds
of followers, ready to back him in whatever
he might undertake.

At the period of our history, the Captain,
discouraged by two or three heavy losses, was
half disposed to secure what remained of his fortune, which, after all his risks and toils, scarcely
exceeded a competency, and to listen to the
earnest entreaties of his only child, a daughter,
now in her nineteenth year, that he would
abandon a mode of life which she abhorred,
as not less disgraceful than perilous, and scrupled not to stigmatize in indignant terms.
That he might have some ostensible pursuit,
and elude the keen suspicions to which his

past life had exposed him, he had some time
before returned to his native haunts, to which
he had always been attached, and hiring a
farm in the New Forest, near Beauley river,
gave out that he had abandoned the free trade,
and meant, in future, to plough the earth instead of the seas for his support. His real
motive, however, for taking the farm-house, a
solid ancient edifice, which had formerly been
a detached grange, appertaining to Beaulieu or
Beauley Abbey, was the accidental discovery
of an extensive range of vaults beneath it,
which had remained hidden and unknown for
several centuries. These he converted into a
store for smuggled goods, concealing the entrance in such an effectual manner, that though
his premises had been repeatedly searched by
the officers, they had never been able to detect
it. This dwelling now constituted his home;
he made no more trips across the Channel,
rarely went to sea, but still carried on the
free trade, although in a narrower circuit,
hoping to redeem his recent losses, and solemnly pledging himself to his daughter, that when

he had done so, he would forswear smuggling, give up the farm, and retire to live at Southampton.

Her mother having died when she was young, and her father having no settled home, Mary, for such was his daughter's name, had been sent to school at Southampton, where she had latterly remained as a lodger, under the care of the same lady who had superintended her education; but when he took the farm, her father, who was doatingly fond of her, brought her home to superintend it, sending her back to Southampton whenever he was obliged to be absent for any length of time. Mary had become much attached to the schoolmistress, who had been as a second mother to her; and it was on this account, as well as that she might effectually withdraw her father from his old haunts and associates, that she had stipulated for his selecting Southampton as his residence, when he should decide upon retiring, a period which she was perpetually imploring him to accelerate.

When the Captain, after leaving the George, arrived at his sequestered dwelling, which still

bore the name of the Grange Farm, it was his
first care to stall and feed his mare; when he
entered the house, noisily welcomed by three
or four mastiff dogs, and passed into a large
low parlour, of which the ceiling was bisected
by a massive beam of oak that had doubtless
once flourished in the woody vicinity, while the
walls were decorated with engravings, all of
which bore some allusion to the New Forest.
There was a smoke-blackened portrait of Henry
Hastings, the memorable keeper and sportsman
in the time of James the First; a view of the
celebrated groaning tree of Badsley, which about
sixty years before had been visited by the
Prince and Princess of Wales, that they might be
ear-witnesses of its portentous sounds;—another
of the Cadenham oak, the rival of Glastonbury
thorn, in budding at Christmas;—a third of
the great yew-tree in Dibden church-yard, and
a drawing of the famous stag which, after
receiving a keeper's shot, collected its dying
energies in a bound that cleared eighteen yards,
a fact commemorated by two posts fixed at
the extremities of the leap in the vicinity of
Hound's-down.

The inmates of the parlour, at the moment
of his entrance, were, first, a short, thick-set,
square-built, bull-headed man, nick-named
Rough-and-ready, a staunch, sturdy fellow,
whose prodigious strength, blunt honesty, and
readiness to apply himself to any work, whether
in farming or smuggling, had recommended him
to the special favour of the Captain, though he
had no talent for plotting or planning, or for
any of the various contrivances requisite to make
an accomplished smuggler; and secondly, a sly-
looking, hump-backed man, called My Lord,
generally employed as a scout or spy, but more
especially retained on account of his wife, a
handsome woman, who formed part of the establishment, and who was highly useful in nego-
tiating bribes with the coast blockade men, or
decoying the officers. These two individuals
appeared to be no otherwise occupied than in
smoking. A boy, called Moon, probably from
the roundness of his vacant face, was gazing
through a telescope at the open window which
commanded the Channel, where it was his business to keep a constant watch, and give information of every thing that he observed.

Reclining upon a chair, and holding a book in
his hand, though with an air of abstraction that
showed he was not reading it, there was another
individual in the room, but oh! how unlike
those we have been describing, and how much
exalted by the contrast they presented! It was
a tall young man, whose symmetry of form was
perceptible even through the homely habiliments in which he had invested it, evidently for
the purpose of disguise; while his fine countenance, in which sorrow and perhaps vice had
made manifest inroads, without having been able
to eclipse its pale beauty, could be compared to
nothing but that of a fallen angel. His redun-
dant glossy brown hair was thrown wildly, and
yet not inelegantly, about his head; his fair
hands, so dissimilar from those of his comrades,
were adorned with rings; and in spite of the
negligence and coarseness of his dress, which was
adapted to the degrading occupation he followed, his suavity of manner, his polished language,
his courteous demeanour, imparted to him a certain air of gentility and distinction, of which the
effect was rather heightened by the deep melancholy in which he was generally plunged. Gen-

tleman George was his common name, although
some of his rude companions, jealous of the
favour shown him by the Captain, bestowed upon
him the less complimentary appellation of George
the Swell. His generosity, indeed, and a courage so reckless as almost to deserve the name
of desperation, had early endeared him to the
Captain ; whose attachment had been strength-
ened by his conduct in a sharp affray with some
of the Preventive Service-men, wherein he had
received a wound in his anxiety to screen and
bring off his leader. In intrepidity and noble-
ness of feeling the two men resembled each
other ; in all other respects they were totally
dissimilar.

For a well-educated, right-principled girl like
Mary, it would have been difficult to imagine a
more inappropriate residence than the Grange-
farm, considering the character and pursuits
of its ordinary inmates. Even with her own
father, however strong might be her filial affection, she did but partially sympathise, for the
coarseness of his manners sometimes repelled
her, while she was at once alarmed and revolted
by the lawless tenor of his life. George, it is

true, was a similar delinquent, but this appearing in his case to be the result of some stern necessity, not of choice, it rather provoked pity than censure. Secluded from other society, she beheld in him the only inmate of the farm whose education and taste assimilated in the smallest degree with her own; the mystery that attached to him, the profound sorrow of which he was the victim, the contrast offered by his fine form, gentle manners, and cultivated mind, to those of his associates, presented themselves to her in a romantic point of view, that could not fail to strike the imagination of a girl so circumstanced; and when we add that he played at times upon Mary's guitar, and sang plaintive love-songs with a most touching melody, it may be hardly necessary to state, that he had completely won her heart long before she suspected that she had lost it. More than once had he given her reason to believe, though not in any direct declaration, that he was fervently attached to her; but upon this interesting point his conduct was so wavering and even contradictory, that she could form no conclusion as to his real wishes; an uncertainty which agitated her feelings, without diminishing the tenderness of their nature.

Scarcely had the Captain entered the parlour, when Mary, having heard his arrival, ran into the room to receive his embrace, which she returned with as hearty a cordiality as it was bestowed; her profuse black locks falling over her glowing face as he roughly saluted her. Although comely, if not handsome, she bore a marked resemblance to her father; every trait of her countenance being, of course, softened and harmonized, and the round, lion-like eyes of the sire expressing only a becoming decision and firmness in the child.

" What cheer, girl?" cried the father, again kissing her with a loud smack; " not sorry to get home again, and in time for dinner, I can tell you that, Polly; for I was at Swanage Bay when the sun rose this morning, and never unshipped bit till I got to the George at Thaxted, where I was obliged to give Black Bess a feed and a rest. George, boy! what makes thee always so down in the mouth? Oh! no wonder; thee 'st been reading, I see, which is but dull work for a brave man. Start 'my timbers!

I never read nothing but invoices and bills of lading, and what's the upshot? I 'm always taut, and braced gaily up. All right, Rough-and-ready?"

" Ay, ay, master, all right. The cages are set, and if we do but get beaks enough, we shall soon clap the sparrows into them."

This piece of slang, which we do not pretend to translate, since the smugglers are constantly changing their vocabulary, and have new pass-words for almost every fresh adventure, seemed to afford satisfaction to the Captain; who next addressing My Lord, inquired whether he had planted his potatoes agreeably to the orders he had received.

" They have been upon the look-out these three hours," answered the hunch-back; " not an oar can move nor a foot stir without their blowing the balloon. Who 's to be spots-man?* and where 's the shy?"

" Time enough to know that, My Lord, when we come to the start. Hallo! Moon, ahoy! look out, platter-face, and tell me what

* The man who fixes the *spot* where the smuggled goods are to be landed.

you see at the Jack-in-the-Basket, off Lymington."

"I see a row-boat that seems to be moored to
the buoy, and two men in her."

"Start my timbers! two men in her! that's
a lie, I'm sure; unless your telescope sees
double; and that's another lie, for it's the best
in all Hampshire.   Give us the peeper."

His own practised eye discovered instantly
that there was but one man in the boat, and
returning the glass to the boy, with the observation that he had either got no eyes, or one too
many, he bade him go and station himself at the
Pigeon-house, charging him not to lose sight of
the Jack-in-the-Basket, and to bring him immediate word when the boat began to move.

Having sent My Lord out of the room upon
some other commission, he shut the door and
window, and observing to his remaining companions, with a wink and a smile, that six ears,
and two of them belonging to a woman, were
five too many for hearing a secret, and that he
was an ass for trusting them, he proceeded to
inform them that the Longsplice, which was the
name of his cutter, would arrive off the coast in

the course of the week, with a valuable crop of
dry goods; and that he had been making arrangements for extensive co-operation in running
them ashore at the breaking of the cliff, about
three or four miles from Hordle, in the vicinity
of which place he had another secret store.

"And I hope, father," said Mary, "this is
the last time you will ever be engaged in such
dangerous and lawless transactions. How often
have you promised me—"

"What do you mean, girl, by lawless transactions?" interposed the Captain. "Start my
timbers! I never wronged a fellow-creature of
a sixpence in all my life; and my word's good
for a thousand pound on either side the Channel. I honour the King; and if I make war upon
the preventive and the blockade, why, it's because they make war upon the free-trade, which
every Englishman had a right to carry on, before these fellows started up. Every body
knows that I did the Government more than
one good service during the war, or else they
wouldn't have granted me the free pardon they
did, and cancelled all the warrants and capiases
against me; and its 'nation hard, if I mayn't

run a crop now and then, which does good to many, and no harm to no one. Howsomdever, if we make a clean job of the Longsplice this trip, without losing a hoop or a halfpenny, I don't know but what I may strike flag, and lay myself up in ordinary."

" Then I 'm sure, father, I shall pray most heartily for your success."

" Who brings over the Longsplice this trip ?" inquired Rough-and-ready.

" Stockings, Ragged Robert, Popgun, and Young Oysters," replied the Captain.

" Ay, ay, all right," growled the other, who was a man of very few words. The boy Moon now came tapping at the window, to say that he saw a skiff making from Keyhaven towards the Jack-in-the-Basket.

" Start my timbers ! a skiff ?—How is she rigged, boy ?"

" Cutter-rigged, with a jib and boom."

" Why then, as sure as ever I 'm standing here, that must be Skeleton Jack out of Lymington. Come along, Rough-and-ready, we shall soon know if it's his skiff, by the red streak ;" and so saying, they hastened to the pigeon-house, which being the highest point on the farm, not only enabled them to make better observation of what was passing, but to hoist certain telegraphic signals for the guidance of their confederates at sea.

" Good heavens !" ejaculated Mary, as they quitted the room, " what a harassing, dangerous, and disreputable life does my infatuated father persist in following !"

" Horrid !" exclaimed George, with a deep sigh.

" I beg your pardon," cried Mary, recovering her recollection at the sound of his voice; "my anxiety for my dear father, made me forget that you were following the same career, or I should not so harshly have condemned it. And yet you termed it horrid. Why, then, do you pursue it ?"

" Oh! do not ask me, Mary; do not turn my thoughts inwards upon the hideous spectacle of myself, for ' that way madness lies.' Why do I pursue it ?" he exclaimed in a louder voice, starting into one of those bursts of vehement passion which were perpetually alternating with his fits of profound dejection—" Why do I pursue it? Because I am a wretch, a reprobate, a forlorn, abandoned, hopeless outcast from the world! Oh, Mary, Mary! I have found more peace—no, peace will never more be mine;—more solace of my incurable anguish in this life of hardship and peril, than ever I have experienced amid bowers of luxury, and scenes of extravagance and riot. And yet even here, in this comparative state of relief, have you not seen how miserable, how wretched, how heartbroken I have been. Oh, God! have I not cause enough for my despair? To know that I was born with prospects of wealth, respectability, and happiness; to feel that I was destined by heaven for nobler pursuits, and higher purposes; to reflect that I have sacrificed my youth, wasted my health, perverted my talents, alienated and embittered my friends; that my short career has been maddened by dissipation, by folly, by crime; and that, now driven from society, degraded in my own opinion, as well as in that of others, I am condemned to lead the life of an outlaw—

"To hovel me with rogues, and swine forlorn,
In short, and musty straw."

Oh, forgive me, Mary! I know not what I say.
Not to your brave and generous father could I
allude; not to any abode in which you are a
dweller: you, who have filled me with mingled
thoughts of happiness and despair; you, who
have at once soothed and tormented my heart;
you, alas! of whom I have only been able
to think with unalloyed pleasure in my
dreams."

"I can easily forgive you, George, for I
never reflect upon the disgraceful purposes to
which our dwelling is applied, without sharing
your own feeling of humiliation at being one of
its inmates. I see, however, by your agitated
and desponding looks, that you have not forgiven yourself. But what could you mean
by saying, I had filled you with thoughts
of despair; that I had tormented your heart?
Indeed, indeed, George, nothing could have
been farther from my wishes and intentions."

"Generous, kind-hearted, Mary! I believe
it—I feel it, and this it is that aggravates my
regret, my anguish. Do not ask me to explain
myself; I must not, dare not! Trouble not

yourself about such a castaway as I am; but
leave me to pursue to its end, (and God grant
that it may be a speedy one!) my wretched
and dishonourable career."

"Why should it continue to be either
wretched or dishonourable? You are young,
you may redeem your early errors; sincere re-
pentance may atone even for your crimes, if
such you have committed, and a future life of
virtue and respectability—"

"Forbear, oh! in pity forbear, to tantalize
me with a delicious dream that can never be
realized. There is no redemption, no happiness in store for me. My follies are irre-
mediable."

"Not all, George, surely not all. Might
you not, for instance, withdraw yourself from
this life of lawlessness and peril?"

"Peril! It is its danger in which I delight.
Oh, if you knew the fierce, gloomy joy with
which my bosom pants when I find myself in
the midst of flying bullets and deep darkness,
in the desperate hope that some friendly ball
may find its way to my heart, and still its
throbbings for ever! And why should I con-

tinue to live? Who would regret me? Every body spurns, repudiates, hates me!"

" Oh no, George, no! Does not my father love you, do not I love you?"

" You love me!—*you!*" exclaimed George, striking his hand upon his forehead—"oh! gracious Heaven! this is the keenest pang, the most dreadful trial of all."

Unaccustomed to measure and weigh her words, the artless girl had merely meant to say, that she shared her father's respect and esteem for their inmate; but instantly conscious of the different interpretation that had been given to her expression, she stood utterly abashed, blushing from brow to bosom, and so confused as to be unable for the moment to explain herself.—" Surely, Sir," she at length faultered, as she held her head proudly up, and shook back the black ringlets that had fallen over her face—" you understand my meaning? I have the same regard for you that my father has;—is it not proper that his friends should be mine? This was what I meant to say, nothing more whatever."

" Heaven knows that I deserve nothing

more ! And yet, if the fond wishes of my heart, this fluttering heart, which is ready to leap out of my bosom at the thought, could be realized—but no, no, no—there is no such happiness for me ! I am doomed to hopeless misery and degradation." The wretched man again struck his hand violently upon his forehead, and sunk with a deep sigh into the chair from which he had risen.

A pause ensued, of which the still blushing Mary felt the embarrassment ; but not knowing how otherwise to escape from it, she snatched up her guitar, and tendering it to her companion with a sportive look, exclaimed :—

"Come, George, away with these gloomy thoughts ! What ! can neither my smiles nor my entreaties gladden that melancholy face ? You shake your head mournfully. Nay, then, you shall not continue in this sad mood. Positively you shall sing yourself into a more happy feeling, for we may sometimes dissipate sorrow by the sound of our own voice."

As he fixed upon her a look at once empassioned and desponding, the tear glistened in his eye ; he took the guitar, and in plaintive

tones, that seemed, indeed, to come from a
stricken heart, thus complied with her request.

" Oh ! turn away, in pity turn
    Away from me that fatal smile ;
It does but make my bosom burn
    With grief that nothing can beguile.
The charms that I can ne'er forget,
    I know that I can ne'er obtain.
Oh ! would that we had never met,
    Or that we ne'er might meet again !

Such fascinating power is thine,
    That tho' I feel 'tis mad to stay,
And doat on what must ne'er be mine,
    I cannot tear myself away.
But do not, do not smile—and yet
    My heart would break with your disdain—
Oh ! would that we had never met,
    Or that we ne'er might meet again !"

Scarcely had he concluded, when the hoarse
voice of the Captain was heard, exclaiming,
as he tapped impatiently at the window :—
" Start my timbers, George ! are you cater-
wauling here along with Polly, when there's a
strange skiff upon the sly off the Jack-in-the-
Basket ? Come along, man, and see what you
can make of her with the Pigeon-house peeper."

This summons was immediately obeyed, and
Mary, now left in the parlour by herself, remained agitated and bewildered by contending
emotions. Her eager explanation of the incon-
siderate phrase into which she had been betrayed, had by no means removed her glowing
confusion, while the tender tone, the impas-
sioned looks, and above all, the love-breathing
sentiments uttered by George in his song, so
much more pointed and explicit than any that
had been previously addressed to her, had set
her bosom heaving, and filled her with tender
thoughts, at once pleasing and distressing. It
was delightful to her, to believe that she had
awakened a reciprocal passion in a man who,
notwithstanding the errors of his former, or the
degradation of his present life, was not only
brave, generous, and accomplished, but one
who had evidently been born and had moved
in a sphere infinitely superior to her own. Perhaps there is nothing more flattering to a female
of comparatively humble station, than the homage of a man thus circumstanced; and if, as
in the present instance, personal advantages and
every winning endowment be added to the

accidental grace of birth, there are few hearts
that can resist the combination. Mary felt that
hers had not been proof against such dangerous attractions. · Whatever George might have
been, she believed that a virtuous woman's love
might redeem him, might reclaim him from his
present evil courses, might eventually save him
from destruction; a conviction that sanctified
her affection into a sort of duty; whilst she
perhaps felt too great a confidence in the ques-
tionable dictum that a reformed rake makes the
best husband. But the more her own feelings
became undeniable to herself, the less could she
account for George's contradictory phrases and
ambiguous conduct. Why all this vacillation
of passion, this fierce struggle against his own
apparent wishes? Why not come manfully
forward and avow his attachment, if he really
felt it? Alas! thought Mary to herself, how
do I know, after all, that he *is* attached to me?
This idle song, from which I would draw such
vain conclusions, was doubtless written by
some distant bard for a different mistress, and
has probably been sung to hundreds of silly,
credulous girls besides myself. As this con-

viction stole over her mind, she heaved a deep
sigh, she felt oppressed by a mingled feeling of
humiliation and disappointment, and, in the un-
consciousness of her reverie, took up the book
that George had left upon the chair when he
had been so hastily summoned away. It opened spontaneously where a paper had been
placed within it, upon which she beheld some
pencil lines in George's well-known hand-writing. They were the words of the song he had
just been singing to her, so altered and inter-
lined, as to show that it was manifestly his own
composition; while the verses, which appeared
to have been left unfinished, were headed with
the words, "Stanzas to Mary."

The fluttering of her heart, the trembling
of her whole frame, the deep suffusion of her
face, attested the sudden agitation into which
she was thrown by this unexpected discovery.
Her eye again hurried confusedly over the
words, without exactly comprehending their
import, or indeed seeing them distinctly; but
as she went over them a second and a third
time, she became enabled to comment upon
them in an eager whisper. " 'I know that I

can ne'er obtain—' How does he know that?
—what does he mean?—' And doat on what—'
—He loves me, then—George *does* love me! He
says ' he doats on me!" —'Ne'er might meet
again!'—Why should he express this cruel
wish?   What prevents —" At this instant
she heard footsteps approaching, and in her
first surprise and alarm, hastily crumpled up
the paper and thrust it into her bosom; but in
the next moment, recollecting the conclusions
that George might draw if he imagined her to
have taken it, she smoothed it out again in a
violent hurry, and replacing it in the book,
rushed out of the room to her own apartment,
crimsoned with blushes, and almost breathless,
from the united rapidity of her flight and the
vehemence of her emotions.

CHAPTER IX

—— Ha! ha! false to me? to me?—
Avaunt! begone! thou hast set me on the rack:
I swear 'tis better to be much abused,
Than but to know a little.

                                                    SHAKSPEARE.

WHILE the Captain took good care to keep
his farm in a proper state of cultivation, that it
might afford the better cover for his real pursuits, he contrived to render it subservient in
various ways to the more important business of
smuggling. The borderers upon the New
Forest are so subject to the depredations of the
neighbouring deer, when these animals have
once gotten a haunt of their corn-lands, that
they are often obliged to burn fires all night for
the purpose of driving them away. By light-
ing these at certain hours, and in particular
quarters, the Captain made them answer the
additional purpose of affording signals to his

confederates at sea; while another expedient
was devised, for those seasons of the year when
such beacons could not be kindled without ex-
citing suspicion. It has been mentioned that
there was a pigeon-house attached to the farm,
situated upon a little eminence, and used as an
observatory. Around the bottom of the beam
that supported it, had been constructed a cir-
cular apartment, with glazed windows, for the
ostensible purpose of serving as a smoking and
drinking-room, but in reality, that when the
Captain and his comrades were carousing in it
at night, they might convert it into a species of
telegraph, by dividing the light by means of
shutters, or leaving it open, for the guidance of
their friends afloat, who could see and interpret
this notice from different parts of the coast.
Near the centre of the knoll upon which this
out-building stood, was a clump of wild, forlorn-
looking trees, consisting of a feeble, shattered,
withered oak, that had been apparently struck
by lightning; two or three bald-topped, meagre,
decaying elms; and a large spruce-fir, some of
whose branches had been torn away, as if by
the same thunderbolt that had scathed the oak,

while the remainder hung ragged and drooping
on one side, waving mournfully in the breeze,
like so many singed and tattered banners.
Springs oozing from the bottom of the knoll
had worn themselves a channel around three of
its sides, the runnel itself being hidden by
bushes and underwood, although its course was
betrayed by its gurgling noise, as it fell from
one little stony ledge to another. Landward,
the pigeon-house commanded an extensive view
of noble forest scenery; while in the opposite
direction it afforded an uninterrupted prospect
of the coast and sea.

To this spot, on the second morning after the
conversation detailed in our last chapter, Mary
had betaken herself with the intention of speaking to her father. He had quitted it, but she
found George plying his telescope from the
window of the smoking-room, or the summer-
house, as she always preferred calling it.
Though not altogether free from embarrassment
or agitation at meeting him, for it was the first
time they had encountered since she had perus-
ed the verses addressed to herself, and which,
during a great part of the night, she had been

endeavouring to recollect and repeat, she tried
to conceal her confusion as much as possible,
but she was still so uncollected, that, after
having quitted the room with her companion,
she almost unconsciously turned as he turned,
and found herself walking up and down with
him upon the turf. When our inward feelings
occasion any delicacy or difficulty in the choice
of a topic, we naturally betake ourselves to external appearances; and Mary, in order to break
a silence, rendered more painful by her companion's evident depression of spirits, observed,
that she loved to linger about the summer-house
on account of the beauty of the view, which she
had seldom seen to more advantage than at the
present moment.

"I, too, find a melancholy pleasure in visiting
this spot," said George, "for I see in it many
objects that remind me of my own fate. Like
this oak, my hopes are all withered and blasted;
I feel myself perishing, like these leafless elms
at top," and he struck his hand to his forehead;
"and yonder forlorn fir, smitten with prema-
ture decay, does but too painfully recal my
own unhappy doom. Nay, as if every thing

that surrounds me were destined to turn my
thoughts upon myself, I am reminded by this
brawling runnel that my own dark and turbulent
career will eventually dash me to pieces over
some precipice, or occasion me to be lost and
buried in ignoble obscurity."

" If you were but in a fit frame of mind,"
said Mary, " you would draw much more
cheerful than desponding images from the face
of Nature. To do this, however, you must be
at peace with yourself, and *that* you can never
be while you pursue this illegal and disreputable
occupation. Oh, that my father and yourself
would both abandon it !"

Abstracted by his own remorseful thoughts,
he had not heard her observation, and pointing
to the plot on which they stood, which happened
at the moment to be involved in deep shade, he
continued,—" Once more does this knoll remind
me of myself; for I, too, am under a dark cloud,
and Heaven only knows whether it will pass
away without pouring forth its thunder upon
my head. I care not—I care not: indeed, I
could wish to be the instant victim of its fury,
if so I might be at peace."—As he spoke, the

sun suddenly darted its streaming rays from
behind the cloud, still leaving the eminence
upon which they stood, and the nearer landscape
in shade, but illuminating the tufted tops of the
forest as it rose amphitheatrically in the distance, and sending fragments of green light
into its glimmering lawns and glades. " Look,
look !" exclaimed Mary; " how beautiful,
how glorious! Does not Nature herself bid
you hope for better and brighter days, by
showing you, that though the present be
shrouded in gloom, the future may be lighted
up with brilliancy and sunshine ?"

" It *is* beautiful—it *is* full of cheering and
consoling suggestions," cried her companion,
while a languid smile passed over his pale, jaded
countenance. " Oh, Mary! Mary! if I could
only say with Burns, that the light which led
me astray, was " light from heaven. "

" Say it not with Burns, nor with any one
else, for no light that really comes from heaven
can ever lead man astray. Yonder glow of ra-
diance is indeed a celestial one; it comes not,
however, to lead you astray, but to beckon you
to virtue; to fill you with the exhilarating con-

fidence that the coming days shall be better and
more cheerful than those which now o'ershadow
you."

"Would I might believe it! would I might
believe it! And why should I not? why may
I not lend myself to the sweet and soothing in-
fluences of this forest, within whose silent recesses I have felt more of the solemn awfulness,
the tranquillizing sublimity of religion, than ever
visited my heart amid the proud domes built
by human hands. Oh! there is no temple like
a natural grove, where the columns have been
reared by an immortal Architect, and into
which the Deity seems to be looking down from
the glorious roof of azure with which he has
overhung it. I have stood, here in this forest
have I stood, in the midst of such a sublime
fane, lost in silent ecstasy, gazing upon the
figures in the evening sky, imagining them to
be the spirits of the departed, who have escaped
from all the troubles of earth, and wishing myself to be floating peacefully among them, until
I have forgotten you, and the world, and even
the sense of my own incurable miseries."

"These, George, are ennobling thoughts,

and feelings which you would do well to encourage. I am only amazed that you can
entertain such elevating impressions, and yet
pursue the degrading career in which you are
now engaged."

" What avail these higher and more holy
promptings of a spirit originally destined perhaps for better things, but now irretrievably
sunk and lost? How can I obey its yearnings,
how listen to its whisperings? Whither can I
go, where hide my head, in what unfathom-
able abyss bury and smother up my shame?
Ask me not what it is—be content to know
that—

" Mine was th' insensate, frenzied part,
   Ah! why should I such scenes outlive!
Scenes so abhorrent to my heart,
   'Tis thine to pity and forgive."

" If they are now abhorrent to your heart ;
if you have indeed repented of them, every one
should pity and forgive them, and above all, you
should forgive yourself. For my own part, I can
never, never believe any man to be irreclaima-
ble to virtue who retains the fervour of his first

attachment to poetry, and I know that you are
still an occasional votary of the Muses."

" Me ! how can you know this ?"

Mary, who had quite forgotten that
George was not aware of her little discovery
about the song, blushed deeply and was confused ; but her companion, not noticing her
embarrassment, continued—" If you allude to
the lines I have just quoted, they are not my
own, but from Burns; whose beautiful poetry
I perhaps admire the more, because I have
sometimes imagined that there is a degree of
similarity in our faults and follies, however little
there may be in our respective talents."

" At all events, it is a miserable waste of
your life as well as talents to throw them away
upon the lawless and ignoble occupation of a
smuggler. Oh that this night's adventure may
succeed, that so my father may redeem his
pledge to abandon it for ever! In that case,
would you not follow his example ?"

" I know not, I care not : joyfully, yes, yes,
gladly, if I might only accompany you in your
retreat. Oh! if I had any one fair and good as
you are to cheer and counsel me, to guide me from

error, to confirm me in virtue, to be the companion and delight of my remaining years—but, no, no, no! there is no such happiness for me—it is impossible, quite impossible, and it is worse than madness to dream of it!"

Not knowing what reply to make to these passionate and perplexing declarations, which seemed to admit an attachment, and deplore some inexplicable difficulty that rendered it impossible to be gratified, Mary was preparing to take her departure in some confusion, when she saw Rough-and-ready pacing his sturdy, measured way towards the Pigeon-house. " What!" exclaimed George, " are you come already to relieve guard at telescope? is it the time we had appointed? I had no idea it was so late."

" Ay, ay, all right," replied the taciturn smuggler, who seldom wasted a word, and who, taking the telescope in his hand, directed it immediately towards Lymington.

" Mary!" said George, joining her as she descended the knoll, and speaking in a low earnest voice, as he looked at his watch; " I have not a moment to lose, I must be absent for two hours, and you will oblige me by not mentioning it to the Captain. It is most vexatious that I must be a truant at such a busy time, and on the morning of such an eventful night as this may prove; but the affair upon which I am engaged is imperative—it concerns my last and dearest hopes, and must not be neglected. I trust the Captain will not notice my absence; I pledge myself that it shall not exceed two hours." So saying, he hastened down the knoll, and struck into the forest at a brisk pace.

Seating herself upon a bench outside the summer-house, Mary remained for some time watching him as he was alternately lost and seen amid the clustering beeches of Boldre-wood-walk, until he turned to the right towards Purley, when, as he was no longer visible, she sauntered thoughtfully back to the house, and took her customary seat at the parlour-window. But she could not pursue her usual avocations; in vain did she endeavour to ply her needle, to amuse herself with her guitar; she sunk into an unconscious reverie, of which George was always the predominant object. The more she reflected upon his conduct, the more extraordinary did it appear. She knew that the cargo

which was expected at night consisted entirely
of silks, to the amount of several thousand
pounds; and that he should absent himself on
the near approach of such an important crisis;
one that, by its result, might determine her
father's future course of life, and perhaps his
own too, seemed doubly marvellous. Still more
inexplicable was it, considering the perfect confidence between them, that he should so anxiously desire his absence to be concealed from
her father, and pledge himself to hurry back
with all possible speed to prevent its being
noticed. His engagement, therefore, whatever
might be its nature, was obviously unconnected
with the night's enterprize, in which he was to
be engaged. He had said that the affair that
called him away was imperative, and could not
be neglected; that it concerned his last and
dearest hopes. As she more than once repeated
these latter words to herself, a vague, uneasy
misgiving arose in her bosom. She recollected
the mystery that involved his fate, the close
reserve in which he had always wrapped himself
up, the contradictory nature of his declarations,
his frequent allusions to some insuperable ob-

stacle that opposed itself to the gratification of
his wishes, and a doubt, a suspicion of she knew
not what, began to agitate her bosom. She was
not without her sex's share of curiosity ; many
motives concurred to interest her most deeply
in every thing that related to George, and in
addition to these stimulants, she reflected that it
was her bounden duty, on such a critical day,
to watch most narrowly the minutest actions of
her father's comrades. Already had he suffered
most extensively from treachery, the constant
besetting danger to which the smuggler is exposed, and to which the temptation was great,
in proportion to the known value of the cargo
to be run. It was the first time that treachery
and George had ever been associated together
in her mind ; even now she absolved him in her
heart from such baseness ; but she wanted a
valid plea, a salvo to her conscience, for endeavouring to penetrate the secret of this mysterious
engagement. She had given a tacit consent
not to communicate his absence to her father,
and this implied pledge she scorned to violate :
but she was bound to nothing more. Appearances were indisputably strange, if not fairly

suspicious; it was due to her father and his other comrades to neglect no measure of precaution; there could not, therefore, be a shadow of impropriety in her following George, and striving to discover the nature of the business which could withdraw him from his friends at this momentous juncture.

So subtle a casuist is the will, that it can presently overpower the clearest judgment, and persuade it that any strong inclination is a paramount duty; under the influence of which process, Mary determined to lose no time in pursuing and watching the operations of her lover, for such he might truly be termed, although he had never made her any explicit declaration of his attachment. Her father had purchased for her a beautiful horse, bred in the forest, and consequently diminutive, but of great spirit and docility, and, like many others of the same hardy race, almost, literally, indefatigable. Without imparting her intentions to any one, she ordered the boy, Moon, to saddle him, mounted, cantered into Boldrewood-walk, and turned into the umbrageous avenue that led towards Purley. From the

frequent habit of riding in the forest, she was
perfectly conversant with—

> " Each land, and every alley green,
>   Dingle, or bushy dell of this wild wood,
>   And every bushy bourn from side to side,"

a circumstance that rather increased than di-
minished the difficulty of her present search;
since, as she had no clue to guide her in her
perquisitions, she had no reason for preferring
one path to another. She rode on, however,
still keeping a general direction towards Purley, but allowing her nag to make his own
choice of the various openings that tended
thitherward, when, after having ridden for
some time, not knowing how she should ac-
complish her design, and yet loth to abandon
it, she beheld through the spray of some tall
underwood a white object on the opposite side
of a small forest-lawn. She stopped suddenly,
for both herself and her horse were effectually
screened by the bushes, and quickly ascertained that the figure was a female, evidently
of genteel station in life, winning her way
slowly and stealthily, and looking anxiously
around, as if she expected to be joined by

some one appointed to meet her. She advanced
half-way across the little lawn, and as Mary
perceived that she was both young and handsome, her heart thrilled with a sickening sen-
sation, immediately after which a burning glow
rushed over her whole frame. A thousand
fears and misgivings flitted like lightning-flashes
athwart her brain, as with a breathless and
intense anxiety she riveted her eyes upon the
figure, which had no sooner come forward
enough to be recognised from an open deer-
shed, at one end of the lawn, than a man ran
out of it to meet her. It was George! He
flew towards the stranger, he embraced her
with ardour, with transport, he placed her arm
within his own, and leading her to the shed,
seated her upon a pile of faggots that had
been left within it, and placed himself beside
her.

Mary was of a vehement and ardent temperament; for a moment she was overcome by
rage and indignation; flashes of light, seem-
ing to sparkle before her eyes, deprived her
for some seconds of all power of distinct vision;
but when she could again distinguish the shed,

she observed that the parties within it were
conversing together with every appearance of
animated and tender interest. It was a hateful, a hideous spectacle, and she again averted
her eyes : indeed she had seen quite enough ;
there could be no doubt of George's infamous
duplicity and treachery, and her wounded pride
quickly gaining the predominance over every
other feeling, she became now solely anxious
to effect her retreat without discovery. She
turned her horse gently round, the turf prevented any sound from his retiring footsteps,
she selected the most umbrageous alley before
her, and had no sooner gained unobserved a
safe distance from the shed, than she struck
her animal with an unwonted sharpness, and
galloped with speed towards the farm, her
face still crimsoned with anger, and her heart
beating with violent pulsations against her
bosom.

It had been her intention to communicate
instantly to her father what she had seen, and
her rapidity had reference to this primary act
of duty ; but as her first ebullient feelings in
some degree subsided, she not only recollected

her promise to George not to betray his absence, but began to reflect that her father was no ways interested in the discovery she had made. Towards *him* there was no evidence of treachery; but as the affair affected herself, it seemed impossible to paint in colours sufficiently black, the atrocious conduct of the delinquent. She had now ascertained the secret object of " his last hopes and dearest wishes;" she had detected the insuperable obstacle to which such frequent and mysterious allusion had been made —he was evidently attached, probably betrothed, nay, perhaps, actually married to the young and beautiful girl whom she had seen in the Forest; and under either of these circumstances that he should attempt, as he manifestly had done, to delude her own affections, and trifle with her tenderest feelings, was an act of gratuitous duplicity, of wanton falsehood, of heartless insult, that filled her with unbounded scorn and indignation. True, he had never made any positive declaration of his love, he had never openly offered her his hand—so much the baser was his meanness and hypocrisy; but had he not laboured to convey the same impression by a thousand equivalent modes, by demeanour, looks, and language, the most expressive, perhaps, when they were the least explicit? For her own part, she was heartily glad that he was unmasked; she had never cared for him, she had never thought of him beyond the passing moment; it was impossible, indeed, that she could have ever bestowed any serious regard upon such a self-condemned profligate and open violator of the laws; and if she felt angry and agitated, it was not that it gave her the smallest concern to throw off the offender for ever, but that she could not advert to his offence without feelings of just detestation and abhorrence.

Thus argued Mary to herself, as, after her return to the farm, she sate in the parlour, endeavouring to work, but only snapping her thread, breaking her needle, unpicking what she had sewed amiss, venting impatient exclamations at her own awkwardness, and immediately repeating the same mistake; when, after she had been for some time thus occupied, the door opened and George entered the apartment. Though flushed and heated from the haste he

had made in returning, there was an unwonted
expression of complacency upon his features,
which Mary, in the momentary glance that she
cast at him, observed, and attributed to the
pleasure he had derived from his recent interview. The thought was not calculated to allay
her feelings, which were again boiling in her
bosom at the presence of the supposed traitor.
Her cheeks burned, her eyes flashed, her veins
swelled, but in the pride of her indignant heart,
she determined to be composed, to affect indifference, and she accordingly fixed her eyes
upon her work, which she plied with increased
diligence.

"I am back, you see, within the two hours,"
said George, extending his watch; "I hope
the Captain has not been apprised of my
absence."

"Indeed, Sir, I know nothing at all about
it," said Mary, speaking in a constrained, unnatural voice, in the unavailing attempt to be
perfectly composed: "at all events, I have not
apprised him. Though I only gave you a
silent promise to that effect, I scorn to violate
it. Thank God! I am no specious hypocrite;

I am no smooth-tongued dissembler; *I* am no habitual dealer in falsehood."

"Good heavens, Mary! what means this strange language? You are angry, what can have happened to offend and disturb you?"

"Angry! disturbed! Oh dear no, Sir, not in the least; I was never more calm in my whole life. I can neither be surprised nor offended at any thing that *you* may think proper to do."

"That *I* may think proper to do! how can *I* have incurred your displeasure? Surely my temporary absence———"

"Nay, Sir, prythee give yourself not the trouble to devise an explanation, which, can only increase the number of your falsehoods, and entitle you the more to my supreme contempt. I will not decoy you into more untruth by pretending ignorance of your proceedings. If the imperative affair upon which you were engaged; if your last and dearest hopes compelled you to make an assignation with a lady in Boldrewood-walk, it concerns not me; and I must beg, therefore, that you will not offend my ears with any of its offensive details."

"O Mary, Mary! have you tracked my footsteps, dogged me through the mazes of the Forest, to discover this secret; and was this worthy of you?"

"I suppose, Sir, I am at liberty to ride where I please; I was on horseback when I accidentally beheld your clandestine meeting," said Mary, condescending to equivocate, as she could not altogether rebut the imputation.

"Mary, you are mistaken: the conclusions you have apparently drawn from what you saw, are wrong, totally wrong. I swear to you most solemnly," he continued, observing that she shook her head with a look of incredulous scorn, "that there is nothing, absolutely nothing whatever in the nature of my acquaintance with that lady which should prevent any other attachment that I might——"

He hesitated, and Mary, striving to maintain an indifference which she was far from feeling, exclaimed in a taunting tone, "Nay, Sir, what you swear, must of course be true; who can doubt it? I have no right to demand any explanation of your conduct, and I am far from wishing to hear it: if you proceed, therefore, it will be for your own pleasure, not for mine."

This speech was made in the hope of stimulating him to some sort of confession, even while she disavowed any desire of the kind; and she was therefore proportionably mortified, when George replied, "No, Mary, no. I must not, cannot follow the dictates of my heart by laying open to you all its wishes, all its hopes and fears. I have sworn secrecy, and whatever may be the consequences, my lips shall be sealed upon the subject of this misapprehended interview. My own safety, and that of another who is still dearer to me than I am to myself, might be fatally implicated by the smallest disclosure."

Mary's warm and impetuous disposition would not allow her to maintain for any length of time a tone of sneer or sarcasm. Frank and straightforward herself, she had a profound hatred of double dealing in others; nor was she by any means scrupulous or measured in the expression of her opinion, when her mind was once made up. In the speech she had just heard, she could perceive nothing but a paltry

equivocation, or a direct avowal that his promise to this unknown lady, and his regard for
her safety, were of greater value in George's
opinion, than any considerations connected with
herself; under the impulse of which irritating
impression, she darted at him a look of ineffable
scorn, as she exclaimed, " Enough, Sir, enough;
attempt not any more evasions; you stand already sufficiently low in my contempt. But I
warn you, once for all, that if you remain beneath this roof, and presume again to address
me in such terms as you have often used, or
in any other than those of the coldest civility,
I shall expose your insidious falsehoods, and
desire my father to chastise and dismiss you
from his house, for having dared to insult his
daughter !"

" I was wrong, I confess I was wrong, if I
have betrayed to you the secret wishes of my
heart ; wishes which should never have been
indulged, because it is impossible they should
be gratified. But, however culpable I may be,
surely, Mary, I deserve your pity rather than
your anger, when I swear to you that the attractions which I have not been able altogether

to resist, have added bitterness to a cup that
was already overflowing."

"I understand not this ambiguous language,"
said Mary, haughtily, "and I will save you
the humiliation of any farther shuffling and
subterfuge." So saying, she hastily quitted the
room, ran up-stairs to her own chamber, and
threw herself into a chair; when her feelings,
no longer sustained by wounded pride and
fierce indignation, presently found vent in an
hysterical burst of tears.

CHAPTER X.

O Heaven, how horrible it is to be
A prey to the wild waters—to contend,
And feel how vain the contest, with the waves,
Th' infuriate winds, and every element
That wars on the wide ocean—to look round,
But look in vain for hope ; and to behold
Fear in the face, and in the soul despair.
                                    G. F. RICHARDSON.

THE Captain, who had been absent upon
some of the arrangements connected with the
night's adventure, now returned, and roused
George from the painful reverie into which he
had sunk, by the hoarse exclamation of—" Start
my timbers ! what are you dreaming on ? Come,
man, be alive, and stir your stumps, for it's
most time for us to be jogging." The party

thus rudely summoned, jumped immediately up,
and proceded to assist his companion in making
preparation for their departure. They looked
out the smock-frocks in which the whole company were to be arrayed—a dress not only ser-
viceable in assimilating individuals, so as to prevent recognition ; but one that had been found
by experience to be less perceptible upon the
sea-shore at night, than any of a darker hue.
The Captain possessed an old-fashioned lum-
bering whiskey, that had apparently been employed for many years in conveying farmers to
market, but which he had procured to be so fit-
ted up with hiding places, secret drawers, and a
false bottom, that he could stow away silks in it
to the value of some hundreds, in such a manner as not to excite the smallest suspicion.   In
this vehicle, drawn by a fast horse, George, accompanied by Rough-and-ready, took his departure towards the coast, carrying with them a
large shaggy black mastiff, known by the unflat-
tering appellation of Belzebub ; probably from
his colour alone, for he shared none of the bad
qualities of his great spiritual namesake. On
the contrary, he was a prodigious favourite with

the whole fraternity of smugglers; but, above
all, with the Captain, by whom he had been
taught to act as occasion might require, either
as a scout, a guard, or an ally; in all which
capacities he possessed the inestimable advantage, in his master's eye, of being the only co-
adjutor, on whose fidelity he could implicitly
depend. My Lord and his wife Nelly, the nature of whose services we have already mentioned, together with the boy Moon, were ordered
to remain, and mount guard at home, and give
signals from the pigeon-house, should any suspicious appearances induce them to believe that
officers were upon the watch in the neighbourhood of the farm. The Captain himself, whose
boyish practice of chasing the wild forest horses,
and throwing himself upon their back without
saddle or bridle, had rendered him a much better horseman than might have been supposed
from the nautical nature of his more recent life,
got ready his favourite black mare; but as he
never quitted home, even on the shortest excursion, without embracing his daughter, and
bidding her adieu, he returned to the house,
shouting " Polly," with his stentorian voice as

soon as he had crossed the threshold. Neither
finding her in the parlour, nor receiving any
answer to his summons, he proceeded to her
room, bolting out, as soon as he beheld her, his
usual exclamation of " Start my timbers, Polly !
what 's the matter ? what are ye piping your
eye about ? has any of our chaps offended ye ?
Tell me who it was, and if I don't bring him
on his marrowbones to ask your pardon, or else
clap a piece of lead in him, unship my rudder ;
that 's all !"

Alarmed at the thought of any dissension between her father and his comrades, which, as
she knew by experience, too often terminated in
treachery, Mary eagerly declared that he was
quite wrong in his supposition ; but that it was
natural she should be cast down, and a little
overcome in spirits, when she saw him about to
depart upon another of those dangerous and disgraceful expeditions which she had so often im-
plored him to discontinue.

" As to disgrace, Polly, that 's all my eye ;
unless the first merchants in Lonnon are dis-
graced : and as to danger, I don't believe
there 's any ; and if so be there should, why,

I 've been too much used to 'em, to mind a few
slashers and barkers. But look ye here, Polly;
ye know I love ye better than any thing else in
the whole world, and can't bear to see ye snivel-
ling—can't upon my soul! so, if all goes right
to-night, as twenty to one it will,—give us your
hand—there!—I promise ye to strike my flag,
and give up the free-trade for ever! There,
girl, now you've got my promise, and Lawrence
Boulderson's bare word is good for five thousand pounds, ay, for ten, upon half a dozen
different exchanges, here and abroad; and there
ain't many a man in England can say that. So
cheer up, Polly; give us a buss, girl, and God
bless ye!"

With these words he left her, mounted his
black mare, and rode towards the coast, taking
a different road from that chosen by his companions, the better to elude observation and suspicion.

During the remainder of this solitary evening, Mary was quite unable to recover her calm-
ness and self-possession; a circumstance which
she attributed to anxiety upon her father's
account, but which might have been assigned,

in at least an equal degree, to her unappeased
resentment against George.　That he should
positively refuse to explain the nature of his
relationship with this strange lady, whose safety
was dearer to him than his own, or his intentions with regard to herself, when an opportunity was afforded him, and when candour and
honesty so imperatively dictated such a course,
convicted him of equivocation and pusillanimity,
even if it did not point at some baser designs
against her own honour.　His conduct at once
irritated her _ feelings, and baffled all her
attempts at its elucidation.　What was the
meaning of all this mystery ; what the motive
for so much inconsistency ; how reconcile his
acts and his professions ?　These problems she
attempted to solve in vain, and when she felt
that every conclusion to which they led her imparted some new pang to her bosom, all her
pride and indignation could not prevent her
from sighing to herself, in the concluding words
of the song she had so recently heard—

> " Oh! would that we had never met,
> 　Or that we ne'er might meet again !"

As these causes of agitation were combined

with considerable anxiety on her father's account, it need not be stated that she felt little
inclination to sleep, even although the usual
hour of her retiring to rest, which was an early
one, had arrived. At this juncture, while she
was pacing up and down the parlour, too much
disturbed in thought to sit still, she heard a
gentle tapping at the door, which was cautious-
ly opened, and the boy Moon, stealing into the
room, told her in a whisper that My Lord was
playing booty, scamping, going to blow the
whole concern. Being asked his reasons for
this alarming conclusion, he added, that he had
seen him covertly hanging a lantern upon one
of the branches of the old oak, on the knoll,
as a private signal; making preparations with
Nelly, that evinced an intention of decamping
from the farm during the night, with all their
effects; and finally, that he had observed him
steal down to the turnip-field gate, and talk to
a strange man, whom he could not distinctly
recognize, but who looked a good deal like
Gentleman George.

Convinced from these and other particulars
that treachery was brewing, Mary, who like her

father was bold, decisive, and energetic, desired
the boy to return and remain at his post as if
nothing had happened; when hastening to the
stable, she saddled and bridled her horse, and
led it slowly round the back of the premises, so
as not to be heard or seen by My Lord and his
wife, who were indeed at this moment too busily
engaged in packing up, to be particularly ob-
servant of what was passing immediately around
them.   Once clear of the farm, Mary's fami-
liarity with all the by-paths and horse-tracks,
enabled her to select such as would effectually
veil her from observation, especially as it was
now deep night, and she accordingly jumped
into the saddle, and galloped fearlessly across
the lonely forest, in the direction of Hordle.
There was no moon, for smugglers seldom execute any of their operations when that luminary
is likely to display her countenance, so that the
forest was wrapped in gloom, save when flashes
of heat-lightning from the distant horizon irra-
diated for a moment the long vistas, or open
lawns and glades, which glimmered before her
in the flitting gleam, and then appeared to be
plunged in tenfold obscurity.   Without this

occasional assistance, however, she would have
experienced no difficulty in finding her way;
and she accordingly proceeded with unrelaxed
rapidity, startling the deer who came out into
the open plots to browze, or scaring their lurking enemy the night-stalker, who, with his toils
and engines, concealed himself in the adjoining
bushes, that he might ensnare and carry off the
fattest of the herd. She passed a fine stag, one
of the " native burghers of the wood," making
pitiable but vain efforts to escape, having been
caught by a hook baited with an apple, and
hung from the bough of a tree. But the forest
was by no means abandoned to the depredations
of poachers and marauders. More than once
she was hailed and menacingly ordered to stop
by some of the under-keepers, apportioned to
the several walks into which that woody district
is divided. On these occasions the mention of
her name, even the sound of her voice, served
as an immediate passport; for however severe
these men might be against poachers, deer-
stalkers, or timber-stealers, neither their duty
nor their interest urged them to take cognizance
of the smugglers. They were, in fact, on

friendly terms with them, but more especially
with the Captain, who had purchased their tacit
connivance by acceptable gratuities; so that
Mary, with only a few of these momentary interruptions, threaded the forest, crossed Lymington River by Battramsley, and approached the
coast in a shorter space of time than could have
been accomplished by any one less conversant
with the country.   Indignation against George
spurred her on to the utmost speed in the hope
of defeating his designs; for having set him
down as a traitor to herself, she believed him
capable of every other atrocity, and guided by
the boy's information, she did not for a moment
doubt that he was perfidious enough to have betrayed her father, and to have given information of the intended landing.   Just before the
morning began to dawn, her anxiety was increased to the utmost degree of intensity. by
the sound of fire-arms, and shouts in the direction of Hordle Cliff; shortly after which she
could perceive several of the light carts usually
employed in running dry goods, driven empty
and at full speed back into the interior, too
sure an evidence that the enterprise had been

discovered and rendered abortive, and that the
country people and others engaged to carry off
the goods were making their escape in all directions.

This was indeed the case. The Captain
had adopted such precautions that nothing but
treachery could have prevented his success.
Always his own *spotsman*, he had fixed upon a
gap near Hordle as the place for running the
goods; the commander of the Longsplice, his
partner in the adventure, was the only person
privy to this determination, until it became
necessary to confide it to the various confederates who were to be assembled at night. At
the dark hour appointed, the Captain, being
provided with a long tube. like a telescope,
lined with polished tin, and containing a lighted
taper, stood upon the beach, placed it against
his body, and moved it gently backwards and
forwards, so that it might be seen from the sea
at a considerable distance, while the light was
utterly invisible from the shore. For this signal the cutter steered, coming as near as the
depth of the water would allow; a low whistle
announced her arrival, the galley loaded with

valuable silks, secured in painted bags to prevent damage from sea-water, was rowed to the
gap, and the men, divided into parties, each of
whose leaders was held accountable to the concern for the number of bags respectively delivered to them, began to unload with incredi-
ble rapidity, and in perfect silence.   Ere the
first boat-load, however, was completely cleared,
a small revenue-cutter ran upon the beach, the
crew jumped ashore, an alarm was given, and
the country people, most of whom had no
deeper interest in the concern than the half-
crown which is usually paid them for their
assistance, and perhaps a small subsequent gra-
tuity when all goes well, fled to their homes
and hiding-places with the utmost precipitation.
The galley was the first object of attack; the
Captain and his remaining comrades making
the most desperate efforts to repel their assail-
ants until they had completed her unlading,
and calling out at the same time to their own
cutter to slip and run instantly to sea.   Regardless of the bullets which now came whistling
around the immediate object of contention, it
was not until the boat was nearly cleared out,

and he was assured that all his comrades were
safely up the cliff, that the lion-hearted Captain
quitted the beach, and mounting his black mare
rode off towards Milford.

Such was the information that Mary received from honest Rough-and-ready, whom she
encountered plodding as unconcernedly inland
as if nothing whatever had happened, and who
had not long before parted from the Captain,
having been ordered to return to the farm. He
added, that since they separated, he had learnt
bad tidings respecting Gentleman George, who,
according to his informant, in attempting to
cover the Captain, had received a shot in the
leg, though it was still believed that he had
managed to make his escape.

"George!" ejaculated Mary—"Was *he*
among you! I had reason to believe that it
was he who had betrayed you all."

"What, Gentleman George!" exclaimed
Rough-and-ready in his turn, with an indignant
surprise,—"Not he, a truer or braver fellow
never smelt powder; he was foremost in the
fray, covered us all, and if I didn't think he
had got clear off, sink me, if I should ever have

left the beach! George turn traitor! No—
no!"—So saying, he pursued his way with his
usual dogged, stubborn look, and Mary, relieved from all immediate apprehensions on her
father's account, continued to advance at a
more leisurely pace, towards the shore, her
thoughts now anxiously reverting, though with
far different feelings, to the supposed traitor.
—Perhaps the heart never yearns so fondly
towards a once cherished object as when we
discover that we have been accusing it un-
justly; in addition to which outbursting of
affectionate remorse, Mary, upon the present
occasion, was agitated with the deepest distress
at the rumour of George's wound, and the probability of his capture. It was in attempting
to rescue or protect her father, that he was stated
to have been shot—a noble self-devotion, that
entitled him to her deepest gratitude, especially as it was the second time that he had
suffered in the same manner. If she had so
cruelly wronged him in this instance, might not
her jealousy have precipitated her into a similar
error, when she suspected him of perfidy towards herself? Might not his conduct, however

mysterious, be susceptible of the most satis-
factory explanation? He swore that it was,
and was it not cruel to doubt him? Generous,
noble, heroic, in his conduct towards her father,
could the same man be false, mean, perfidious,
towards herself? Impossible! She would await
his justification, and she now felt confident that
it would establish his honour and veracity.
Prompted by a secret love which, though it had
been momentarily checked, had suffered little or
no diminution, thus argued Mary, until she,
who had so lately visited George with all the
fierceness of contemptuous indignation, now
thought of him with mingled feelings of peni-
tence, gratitude, and affectionate admiration,
heightened by the keenest anxiety for his safety.
It had been her intention to rejoin her father at
Milford, and as her riding along the coast would
not materially lengthen her route, while it might
enable her to collect some certain information
of George's fate, she pushed forward to the sea-
shore.

The object of her solicitude was, at that moment, not only suffering the extremity of mental
and bodily anguish, but in a perilous predica-

ment, that hardly allowed him a chance of
escaping with his life. In his attempt to screen
the Captain, he had received a ball which had
broken the bone of his leg, notwithstanding
which he had contrived to scramble some little
distance along the shore, and, favoured by the
darkness, threw himself down beneath a crag,
which had been detached from the cliff, and
lay near the water's edge. In this situation he
remained, propping himself against the crag,
and groaning with torture, until the morning
broke, when, upon casting his eyes to the sea,
he could just recognize the cutter scudding
away to the south, and chased by the revenue
vessel, though far a-head of her. No other
vessel was in sight; he was hidden from the
beach; he could hear no sound of voices; all
was silent where but lately all had been clamour
and tumult. Ignorant of his fate, his comrades
had probably left the shore; it was not impossible, however, that some of them might still be
lurking under the cliff, waiting for daylight to
look out for him; and, in order to avail himself
of their services, it was necessary that he should
render himself visible by climbing to the top of

the crag. Easy as it appeared, he found it
impossible to carry this design into execution.
Sick, dizzy, faint with fatigue and the loss of
blood, he found that his powerless limbs refused
to obey him, and, after several ineffectual efforts,
which only aggravated his sufferings, he fell
back into his former position, and resolved to
abandon the attempt. Almost at the same moment, he made the appalling discovery that he
had crawled beneath this fatal rock at low
water, and that the flowing tide, which now
nearly touched his extended feet, threatened
speedily to overwhelm and destroy him !

At the first conviction of this inevitable fate,
the perspiration started in large beads from his
forehead, a sudden and deep flush overspread
his features, which almost immediately resum-
ing their ghastly paleness, wore an expression
of mingled agony and horror. He was naturally
of a resolute and almost undauntable spirit, but
the hopelessness of all succour or escape, now
inspired him with a gloomy despair. Life, however, had long been a burden to him, and now
that he could no longer retain it without the
probability of his being made a prisoner and

exposed to public shame, or the certainty that, even if he were rescued by his comrades, he must undergo some painful operation for his broken leg, perhaps after all to die in miserable anguish, he became in some degree reconciled to his fate, and resolved to encounter his approaching death without flinching, and, if possible, without even a regret. Fixing his eyes therefore upon the advancing waters with a stern composure, his thoughts reverted to all the faults, follies, and crimes of his past life, a retrospect that filled him with compunction and remorse; while the hopelessnes of the future, even if he could escape his doom, left him little to bewail in dying. A pang, indeed, shot through his heart as the image of Mary passed athwart his mind, and he murmured her name with a deep sigh; but such was the cruel waywardness of his lot, that even this, his last, his only chance of happiness upon earth, was rendered unattainable by insuperable impediments. Conscious that his end was approaching, he withdrew his thoughts from all worldly objects, and determining to employ the short space that was yet to be allowed him in imploring forgiveness

of his offences, he fixed his haggard looks upon
the sky, and remained absorbed in penitent and
fervent prayer.

Not so completely, however, could he abstract
his thoughts from the earth, but that he felt an
involuntary shudder as the waters flowed over
his legs, while he imagined that he heard his
death knell ringing with a terrific loudness in his
ears as the waves broke with a plash against the
crag. Every succeeding surge rose higher and
higher, sending a more icy chill to his heart,
and as he mentally calculated to what part of
his frame the next would reach, and how long
it might be before his sufferings would termi-
nate, nature recoiled from a death so appallingly
slow and protracted, and yet apparently so inevitable. While thus gloomily meditating, he felt
the buoyancy of the element which had already
began to enwrap his body, and a sudden flash of
hope shot like lightning through his mind.
By the assistance of the rising waters he might
perhaps lift himself to the top of the little crag.
This too, he was well aware, must be speedily
overflowed by the tide, and in that case he
would only have deferred his wretched fate;

but in the short interval he might be seen by
some of his comrades, he might be saved !

Life is sweet even to the most miserable: his
despair was momentarily chaced away; a new
hope inspired him with fresh energy; instead of
contemplating the waves as his fell, inexorable
executioners, he hailed them as his guardian
angels, his preservers, and buoying himself as
well as he could upon their surface, he succeeded, after the most painful and convulsive efforts,
in dragging himself to the top of the crag, so
weak and exhausted that he lay outstretched
upon its summit, just able to raise up and
wave his right-arm as a signal.

At this critical moment Mary, having reached the summit of the cliff above, threw her
anxious eyes along the beach in the direction
of the Isle of Wight, over the hills of which the
sun had just risen, throwing broad shadows
from its shores, and tipping with a crown of
light the summits of the Needle Rocks. She
could perceive no moving object except some
distant fishing-boats, but as her looks wandered
in another direction, she discerned something
moving upon the crag. At first she imagined

it to be seaweed, blown up by the wind; but on
viewing it more intently, she discovered that it
was a human being, and the instant suspicion
of the truth sent an electrical shock through
her whole frame. It might be, it must be
George, rendered helpless by his wound, and
left thus miserably to perish? Be it whom it
might, not a single second would her generous
heart pause to deliberate. She leapt from her
horse, ran like an antelope down the precipitous
gap, plunged into the waves, hurried to the
crag, and uttering a piercing shriek as she
recognized the agonized features of George,
she fell upon the rock beside him. Conscious,
however, that not a moment was to be lost, she
instantly recovered herself and started up, intending to support and assist him to the shore;
but his blood-shot eyes, his death-like countenance, his faltering, gasping voice, his wounded leg, which had dyed the crag with gore,
superadded to her fatigues during a sleepless
night, and the shock of violently contending
emotions, were altogether too much for her.
Her's was a courageous heart, but after all it
was a woman's; nature was unequal to the

struggle she had previously undergone, and the
hideous, the withering spectacle on which she
was now gazing with looks of horror. The
scene floated dimly before her eyes, a hollow
noise rung in her ears, she murmured a few
inarticulate sounds, and slipped fainting from
the crag.

George had convulsively grasped her hand,
but totally powerless to raise her from the sea,
he was doomed to the unutterable anguish of
seeing her sink into the waters beside him. Her
dishevelled tresses floated around her head;
once—twice—thrice did the waves flow over
her pale lifeless face, as she lay extended like
a beautiful marble statue. He could no longer
bear the heart-rending sight, but with a deep
groan sunk down insensible upon the hand
which he still retained in his unconscious
grasp.

CHAPTER XI.

―――― And for your reading, let that appear
when there is no need of such vanity.

SHAKSPEARE.

HAVING in the first chapter of our work
given a description of the Manor-house, the residence of Justice Welbeck and of his daughter
Emily, we should not so long have withheld
our readers from a visit to it, but that Henry
Melcomb, who was unacquainted with the Justice, and had, therefore, no excuse for intrud-
ing himself unaccompanied, could not easily
persuade Penguin to go with him and introduce
him, although it was his first request that he
would do so. It will be recollected, that immediately upon his arrival at Thaxted, he had
walked over to the neglected, wild-looking park,

and had wandered round the venerable but
forlorn mansion, half of which was shut up,
while the whole wore a still more desolate aspect
from its partial occupancy than if it had been
totally tenantless. What he had seen upon that
occasion, had but the more deeply interested
him in the fate of Emily, cloistered in so
sequestered and gloomy an abode, with a father
whose penurious habits would not allow him
becomingly to enjoy the immense wealth which,
as he was now informed, he had accumulated
by not very creditable means, and whose character, at once violent and hypochondriacal,
seemed to account for that pensive, if not melancholy temperament which he had observed
in the daughter. In Emily it was united with
a bashful, retiring timidity that accorded well
with the style of her beauty, and rendered her
altogether inexpressibly interesting. Although
her face exhibited an habitual paleness, or
rather a blanched delicate hue, more the result
of sorrow than of sickness, it was frequently
suffused with blushes, whose fugitive visits
imparted a still more exquisite grace to the
transparent fairness that succeeded them. A

tear seemed to be not seldom trembling in her mild, dove-like eyes, which were often diffidently cast down beneath the fringe of their long sable lashes; while there was a mournful expression in the slightly-depressed corners of her mouth, and the soft plaintive tones of her voice, that told touchingly of some secret sorrow, endured with resignation, but felt with deep sensibility. At such an age as hers, for she was now in the first bloom of youth, it might be expected that she should be somewhat more sprightly and loquacious, and she had been even reproached by superficial observers with a want of animation; but when her heart was kindled by any noble action, or affecting sentiment, she spoke and looked with an enthusiasm that quickly brought words to her tongue, the blood to her glowing cheek, and the tears of generous sympathy to her eyes.

Henry, as has already been stated, had lodged for some little time in the same boarding-house with her at Southampton, whither she had gone on a visit to a sick aunt. Circumstances had thrown them much together, for the invalid lady had taken a fancy to him, and fre-

quently invited him to join her tea-parties
at home, or the excursions in the beautiful
neighbourhood, which had been recommended
for the benefit of her health. Struck by
Emily's appearance, suffering as she manifestly
was from some concealed heart-grief, and not less
interested in her conversation, Henry had
attached himself to her upon these occasions as
much as was consistent with the avoidance of
such particular attentions as might lead to a
misconstruction of his motives. Had not his
high and honourable *feelings* led *him* to abhor
with a special detestation the character of a male
coquet, another principle would have decided
him not to compromise either his own affections
or Emily's. Must we confess a truth which, in
the estimation of some of our fair readers, may
place him, we fear, in a most unsentimental
light? He was a disciple of Malthus, deep in
the theory of the preventive and positive checks
to population, a subject in which he felt a profound interest, from its importance to the happiness and independence of the lower orders.
No man, in his opinion,- was warranted in
marrying, unless he had a reasonable prospect

of maintaining a family, so that it should not
become burthensome to the community. His
own situation at present afforded him no such
prospect. Emily might be as poor as himself,
for he had then heard nothing of her father's
wealth, having made no inquiries upon the subject, and he therefore considered her as out of the
question of marriage, at least to an individual
so scantily provided as himself, without pausing to consider whether his own feelings or hers,
when exposed to the influence of the passions,
could be always made to square themselves by
the rules of political economists, or the calcula-
tions of cold abstract reasoning.

Young gentlemen, even such as Henry, whom
we should be very sorry to confound with the
vulgar herd of gentility, make bad philoso-
phers; but young ladies can be seldom brought
to philosophise at all. In spite of himself, and
notwithstanding a demeanour that had been
strictly guarded, Henry had unconsciously
awakened a flutter of tender emotions in the
bosom of Emily, who, without adverting to
theories and systems, or sufficiently considering
the sanctions of prudence, listened to his gene-

rous and disinterested sentiments with a moral homage which her sensitive heart soon kindled into personal admiration. This sort of process is amazingly accelerated by a contrast of impressions, at least, where the change is from repugnant modes of action, and revolting habitudes of thinking, to those with which our whole soul eagerly and delightedly sympathises. At home, Emily heard nothing but sordid and grovelling maxims, saw nothing but the grinding oppression of a crafty, covetous, penurious man, constituting the very element in which she was condemned to live, and from which she could only make occasional and stealthy escapes, when the generous dictates of her own heart led her to soften the lot of those who were subjected to her father's exactions, or to any other calamity. This she was often enabled to do more extensively than might have been imagined; for however mean and mercenary he might be to others, towards Emily he was liberal even to profusion; so that she had it in her power secretly to remedy many grievances, and alleviate much of the distress with which the neighbourhood was afflicted.

Though she could thus covertly indulge in
more congenial modes of action, she could never,
in the presence of her worldly-minded father,
give vent to those sentiments of disinterested
virtue and benevolence with which her own
mind was imbued, without being ridiculed as
chimerical, or hearing her opinions stigmatized
as the perilous aberrations of a romantic girl.
Escaping, for the first time in her life, from
such an uncongenial moral atmosphere, and
thrown into the society of Henry, it may be
supposed with what delight and avidity she listened when he expatiated, as he was so fond of
doing, upon those views of enlarged and liberal
philanthropy, which had not for their object any
particular tribe or district, but the melioration
of the whole human race. He condemned that
odious conflict of opinions upon subjects either
unimportant or undeterminable, which only
serves to embitter life; when, by substituting
practice for theory, by performing duties instead of squabbling about idle dogmas, and
indulging in no other rivalry than the generous
race of active benevolence, we might, in a ma-
terial degree, amend the errors of our social

system, and diminish the general sum of misery. To such sentiments every chord of Emily's heart vibrated in unison; in spite of all her efforts to suppress them, the tears of enthusiasm stole down her cheeks, and Henry often attributed to her own secret grief an apparent distress, which was in reality the overflowing of a generous and delighted sympathy.

These affecting meetings were over. Emily had returned to the Manor-house, uncertain whether she might ever again behold the companion of her Southampton excursions, but ever thinking of him, and of his exalted doctrines, with an admiration heightened by the contrast of all that now surrounded her. Her first return increased the general depression of her spirits; but still she did not regret her visit to her aunt: it had furnished her with a store of pleasant and ennobling recollections, which, amid many sources of disquietude and regret, seldom failed to afford her a solace.

Henry, on the other hand, who found his thoughts perpetually reverting to his fair acquaintance, attributed the interest that he took in her fate to compassion at her evident

unhappiness. The young philosopher had yet
to learn that the pity felt for an amiable and
beautiful girl is soon fostered into a warmer
sentiment; a fact which, if he had suspected,
he would not have been so importunate with
Penguin to introduce him at the Manor-house.
Perhaps the *ci-devant* contrabandist felt an
instinctive dislike of a magistrate, who, whatever might be his offences in other respects, was
rigid and impartial in the discharge of his judi-
cial functions. "Gad, my young friend!" he
exclaimed, in reply to Henry's application, "I
like Emily—a sweet girl! rather dumpy and
down in the mouth, as well she may be: but as
to the old curmudgeon, I can't abide him; I
term him a specimen of primitive trap, hey!
Well, well, don't look so glum; I told you I
was a bit of a wag. I had much rather call
when he is not at home; it will be the quarter
sessions soon, when he is sure to be absent: by
that time you will have brought Mrs. Tenby
down from London, and we can then all go
together."

"Pray speak for yourself, Mr. P." said his
wife; "I am by no means sure that I shall

accompany you: it's a horrid gloomy house, makes one quite mopish; and besides, I don't like the daughter much better than you do the father. Instead of throwing away her money upon the good-for-nothing poor, and all sorts of fantastical charities, methinks she would act more becoming her station in society if she were to dress a little handsomer; though, to be sure, it's hardly worth while, with such a mealy face and insignificant little figure. This is the second year she has worn that old-fashioned lilac pelisse." As she concluded this observation, the speaker complacently surveyed in the glass her own substantial form and over-fine dress, which bristled with novelty, while she adjusted her ringlets, in order to display the sparkling rings with which her fingers were loaded.

" And yet nobody ever looks so neat and tidy as Miss Welbeck," observed Penguin.

" Neat and tidy! pray give up these trades-men-like ideas, Mr. P. Why, any shopkeeper's daughter can be neat and tidy upon twenty or thirty pounds a year. With the money that Miss Welbeck evidently has at command, she must be a poor, mean-spirited creature not to cut a greater dash. Why doesn't she dress like me, or Lady Susan, or Miss Frampton? Ay, they carry money upon their backs, and let you see that they know it. As to Fanny Frampton, she's a silly, wild girl, too fond of nonsense and trifles, and perhaps too young to feel the importance of wearing real good things, and none of your plain, cheap, old-fashioned trumpery."

" But what is there about the father that renders him so objectionable?" inquired Henry, who considered the observations levelled against Emily to convey an encomium much rather than a censure.

" What first unhinged the old gentleman's mind, for he was not always thus," replied Penguin, " is a secret which I would give a trifle to know: but the fact is, that he has for many years been subject to sudden fits of passion, and dismal attacks of hypochondria; some say, indeed, that he is at times half mad ; and these symptoms have become so much aggravated since his son disappointed all his hopes and ran away to the continent, that the servants, I am told, are frequently disturbed in the night with his cries

o 3

and groans, though he will allow no one to approach him upon these occasions but his daughter, poor Emily, who sleeps in an adjoining
chamber, that she may be always ready to con-
sole and assist him."

"Oh! he's a horrid old skinflint!" cried the
wife. "Would you believe it, that, though he
is rolling in riches, he hardly keeps any table,
and never makes the least display, though he
has a strong-room in the house cram full of
heavy old-fashioned plate? Now and then it
is raked out when he gives a half-yearly dinner
to his brother magistrates and some of the
neighbours; but it is a sad blundering business,
the things badly dressed, and worse put upon
the table. His wines, indeed, are decent, for
in his possession they are sure to get old!"

"It is sometimes very unpleasant to be in
his company," continued Penguin; "you are
never sure of him, for while he is conversing
agreeably enough, he will all at once stop, and
sink into a stern, moody reverie; or start off
from the subject, and rant as wildly as a moon-
struck tragic actor."

"That which is common," said Henry,

" we have little wish to see; but the being you have been describing is a singular one, and you have therefore been increasing my desire for an interview, while you have been striving to diminish it. Poor Emily! what a melancholy abode! what a painful lot! You will really oblige me by accompanying me this morning to the Manor-house; and besides, I thought you delighted in the developement of character."

" Who?—I! not in the least. Oh! ay, I recollect, all right, all right, so I do, it's quite my hobby-horse, after geology; but I can't go this morning, for you see I have got on 'my vaga-bondising dress, with my wallet and hammer."

" These may be easily changed, and if you would escort me to the Manor-house, we might afterwards visit the bed of shells you were mentioning, which cannot be much out of our road."

" Egad! my young Domine, and so we might. Ay, that stratum runs from the coast quite through the Forest, and what's curious, they 're all tropical shells, and found only in this neigh-bourhood. I can show you a good many of them in my museum, and there are above a hundred and twenty engraved in the Fossilia Hautoniensia, which you can look over while I am changing my dress. But it will be a long round, and my legs are not quite so young as yours; not able to vault across the Miller's-run, hey? so I 'll drive you over in the gig."

"Indeed, Mr. P. you will do no such thing," cried his better half, with a look and tone of great decision: " you will never drive that gig again. Remember how you upset it coming down the hill by Lady-cross Lodge and nearly killed yourself; and how you nearly drowned the horse another day by driving him to drink in the deepest part of Avon-Water Bottom. James shall drive you, and it will besides look much genteeler, for he has got a new livery, and a glazed hat, with a gold-lace band, and there's plenty of room for three in the gig; I had it built roomy on purpose."—Henry declared that such an arrangement was perfectly unnecessary, as he was himself so practised a whip, from having driven vehicles of all sorts in America, that he would be responsible for the safety of his companion."

"Oh! that's another matter!" exclaimed the

lady: "in that case, I can willingly trust him to your care; but poor dear Mr. P. is so perfectly *non compos* when he is thinking about those nasty shells, and dirty, rubbishing bones, that I am determined he shall never handle the reins again. Come, my dear, let me see about helping you to change your clothes. God knows what would become of you, if you hadn't a good wife to look after you, and to care for you!"

"Capital! capital!" whispered Penguin, shrugging his shoulders, and winking to Henry as his spouse left the room: "I proposed driving on purpose, just to try her; knew how it would set her off—you were quite right, I *do* like to draw out people's characters." So saying, he hurried after her, having previously placed in Henry's hands the promised book of engraved fossils, which he thought calculated to beguile a much longer time than he was likely to consume in dressing, for he was brisk and expeditious in all his operations.

Philosophically indifferent as Henry generally was to the fashion and cut of his habiliments, although punctilious in the preservation of an almost quaker-like neatness, he found that, upon the present occasion, his dress required some little improvement; a discovery which would probably have never been made, had he not been about to visit Emily. He proposed, therefore, that they should pass through Thaxted in their way, and stop for a short time at the George; an arrangement to which Penguin gave a willing assent, as it would enable him to enjoy his favourite luncheon of syllabubs and biscuits. On their arrival at this rural caravansary, Sam Ostler, who had a shrewd ear for the sound of a carriage-wheel or a horse's hoof, took hold of Penguin's mare as they drew up, and patting her on the nose, while he surveyed her whole figure, exclaimed, " She be in rare condition, Muster Penguin, baint she? Ay, and as steady a mare as any in all England, I look upon 't, if people can but drive. A little hair off the near knee from that ere tumble down Lady-cross-hill, which is a good ten pound off her value, but she don't seem to have got no sprain from dragging the chay out of Avon-Water Bottom. Heart alive! only to think of your driving her in there!"

"Curse these fellows!" cried Penguin, pettishly; "they fasten as naturally upon a man's
sore places, as the flies upon the raw back of
a horse."

"Sarvant, Sir, sarvant!" cried Tony, who
now ran out, pulling a lank lock of his pig-
coloured hair. "What! Muster Penguin, you
ha'n't got your worky-day dress on this morning;
too hot to break stones, baint it? Bodikins!
that were a prime good one, warn't it, that
trick as Squire Frampton's Blackeymoor sarved
ye down by the Miller's-run and the marl-pit?
Lame Richard and Joe Penfold took a quart
here last night, and told we all about it. How
us did laugh, sure-*ly*! I'd ha' stood a pint to
see the Black fellow making mouths at ye from
the alder bushes, danged if I oodn't!"

"Confound your jabbering!" cried the geologist, with a look of offended dignity: "Shut
up your own ugly mouth, or you'll never see
another sixpence of mine." So saying, he
passed hastily into the house, followed by
Henry; while Tony, pulling his features into
a grimace, and putting his bony finger to
his nose, looked at Sam with such a ludicrous

distortion, that the latter was obliged to stoop
and hide his face behind the mare, lest his
chuckling visage should be seen from the parlour-window, to the diminution or total for-
feiture of his expected groat. Henry ran up-
stairs to make the requisite alteration in his
dress, and Penguin, having inquired after Sally,
and ordered some syllabubs, provided they were
prepared by her, and not by crooked Martha,
proceeded to make his usual inquiry of the
landlord, who came bustling into the room, of
what news was stirring at Thaxted. "News,
Sir!" exclaimed Timothy: "Bless us! such
a life as I lead here at the George, toiling
and moiling from morning to night, I have no
time for news, not I. Just snatched half an
hour last night to run over to our 'sociation,
and hear a bit of a lecture upon chemistory;
but he was a poor creature, quite a borax of a
fellow; couldn't catch his focus; never came
right slap bang, point-blank, plump upon the
fulcrum, like Professor Pully, but all our-
vilinear and gelatinous like, and if it puzzled
me I'm sure he must have finely bothered the

hopperatives who were present, for instead of acting upon the equilibrio, he was always in a state of osculation. Couldn't fix him no-how.—Why, what are Sam and Tony snigger-ing at yonder? There's always some secret coagulation going on 'twixt those two.—What bell was that?—Tony! Tony, I say! cold meat, tankard ale, Gemman, Dolphin. Coming, Sir, coming!"

" But surely, landlord," said Penguin as he assaulted his second syllabub, " you must have picked up something new at the lecture, how-ever short a time you stayed."

" But little, Sir, but little: couldn't make out his trigonometry; never gave him a mini-mum of attention till he mentioned ox-hides of iron! Don't tell me: I hold it as a vertical truth, a mathematical maximum, that ne'er a tanner in England can make them as hard as iron! Odds life! I had a mind to give him a hint that the shoemaker should stick to his last, when he went into a comic section about hydro-gin and oxygin, for I 've kept a tap these twenty years, and I know there 's none equal to Booth's best. Only think of people lecturing when they know nothing about the density and diameter of what they 're talking of!"

" Ay, that 's bad enough, landlord, but we must make allowances; your society is but newly established, and cannot yet afford to have the best lecturers."

" Very true, Sir, very true; we can't all be equally learned, for the impetus must depend upon the circumference. I don't wish to be hard upon the gemman, for give and take 's my maximum—nothing diagonal about Tim Wicks, all upon the square root, straightforward as a parallelogram; but how can I sit still and hear a chap talk about sugar of lead, and salt of lead, when I must know more of the trigonometry of them things than he does; for father were a plumber, and melt or hammer his lead which way he would, I 'll swear he never got sugar or salt neither but what came from the grocer's! He may talk till he 's black in the face about malleability, and fusibility, and friability, ay! and roastability if he likes, but he can't have a segment, no, not a tangent of real ability, which after all, is the only solid hydrostatical fulcrum!

Sam Ostler! draw off gig, Lymington coach driving up—water horses. Coming, Sir, coming!"

" I don't wonder, Tim, that you soon came away, since there was so little to be learnt, and your time is so precious."

" Why, Sir, to tell you the vertical truth, I had half a mind once to stay till the end, on account of poor crooked Martha, my inclined plane, as I call her—d' ye catch the focus, hey?—for as he talked about empy-rheumatic oil, I thought I 'd step and ask him for a shilling's worth, since Martha, poor soul! is sadly troubled with the rheumatiz all over her whole hemisphere. But he went on to humbug us, that a diamond was made of charcoal, which appeared to me such a downright false pivot and sham segment, that I clapped on my hat, bolted out of the room, and as Bat Haselgrove was driving by at the moment in his taxed-cart, I jumped into it, he drove me over to the George, and sat me down right slap bang point blank, plump upon my own fulcrum."

" Gadso, landlord! that was lucky; but have you no other news than this? you have gene-

rally some of the chit-chat of Thaxted to tell
me."

" Why, Sir, the great first principle and pri-
mum mobile with us at present is this here fair,
which we mean to make a grander one than has
been seen here for many a year, and if the
gentry attempt to put it down by inert force,
we are determined to stand up boldly for our
own inverse ratio. No, no, we're not such
gudgeons as to be caught with an angle of
forty-five degrees; their opposition will only
enlarge our axis; and this must ever be the case
in a free country like ours, since the percussion
is alway proportioned to the area—d' ye catch
the focus, hey ?"

Before Penguin could reply, a carriage drove
up to the door, and the landlord ran out of the
parlour, calling in the same breath for Tony,
Sam Ostler, and Sally Wicks, and muttering to
himself a *da capo* about his bustling life, no
peace, toiling from morning to night, &c. &c.
Penguin had by this time dispatched his syllabubs, a process, indeed, which had been going on
uninterruptedly during the whole of Timothy's
catachrestical gabble ; Henry shortly after re-

appeared, when mounting their vehicle, they proceeded towards the Manor-house, into which mansion we shall take the liberty of introducing our readers, while the geologist and his companion are driving thither.

END OF THE FIRST VOLUME.

LONDON:
PRINTED BY S. AND R. BENTLEY,
Dorset Street, Fleet Street.

Lightning Source UK Ltd.
Milton Keynes UK
UKHW020628260722
406393UK00005B/765